TOMORROW* AND *TOMORROW

"Millar excells . . . .Superlative!"

—Publishers Weekly

"Her writing is a delight of clarity and pungency . . . tantalizing . . . exciting."

—Saturday Review

"One of our best writers."

--Philadelphia Inquirer

D1431225

Novels by **MARGARET MILLAR**
available in Crime Classics ® editions:

MARGARET MILLAR

Ask For Me Tomorrow

LIBRARY OF CRIME CLASSICS®

MISTER E'S™

INTERNATIONAL POLYGONICS, LTD.
NEW YORK CITY

To Charles Barton Clapp

ASK FOR ME TOMORROW

Text copyright © 1976 by Margaret Millar. Introduction copyright
© 1985 by Margaret Millar and Kenneth Millar 1981 Trusts. Reprinted
with permission of the author and Harold Ober Associates, Inc.
425 Madison Avenue, NY, NY 10017.

Library of Congress Card Catalog # 91-73853
ISBN 1-55882-115-5

Printed and manufactured in the United States of America.
First IPL printing April 1985.
New edition November 1991.

10 9 8 7 6 5 4 3 2 1

INTRODUCTION

Most books are knitted, stitch by stitch, starting with a skein of yarn and a pair of needles. Others are made of whole cloth and all the author has to do is add some pleats and piping and deep mysterious pockets, and there is the book, complete in a way the knitted book rarely is.

I knit my books, (Dare I say, casting purls before swine? Probably not.) I unravel, change yarns, drop a few stitches here and a few there, until the garment is finished.

ASK FOR ME TOMORROW is the only book of mine that was truly made of whole cloth. The plot came to mind in its entirety. I added some false flounces and portentous plicature, and the resulting garment was exactly as I had planned when I wrote the first sentence.

Sticking to one's knitting can be tedious. The writer presented with a whole piece of cloth is lucky indeed. So is the reader.

M. Miller

Santa Barbara, CA
April 6, 1984

Ask for me tomorrow and you shall find me a grave man.

Romeo and Juliet
Act iii, Scene I

One

It was late afternoon. As Marco dozed in his wheelchair the long lazy rays of the sun touched the top of his head and stroked the sparse gray hairs of his good arm and fell among the folds of his lap robe. Gilly stood in the doorway and watched her husband, waiting for some sign that he was aware of her presence.

"Marco? Can you hear me?"

Only a few parts of his body were capable of movement and none of them moved. No spasm of the fingers of his right hand which operated the controls of his wheelchair, no twitch of one side of his mouth, no flutter of his right eyelid, which was the one that opened and closed normally. The other eye remained as it always did, the lid half open and half closed, the pupil dead center. Even when he was awake no one could be sure exactly what he was looking at or how much he saw. Sometimes Gilly thought the eye was accusatory, staring directly at her, and sometimes it seemed amused as if it were focused on some wry joke in the past or bit of fun in the future. "It sees nothing," the doctor had told her. "But I'm sure you're mistaken, Doctor. It *looks* at things." "The eye is dead."

The dead eye that saw nothing watched Gilly cross the room. She made no noise. The carpet was silent as grass.

"You're pretending to be asleep to get rid of me, aren't you, Marco? Well, I won't go. I won't go, see?"

See? The dead eye didn't, the live one stayed hidden under its lid.

Gilly touched her husband's forehead. It was scarred with wrinkles as if some cannibal had started to eat the flesh, had dug his nails across it leaving tracks like a fork.

"It makes me nervous when people pretend," Gilly said. "I think I'll scream."

She didn't, though. Whenever she screamed, Marco's nurse, Reed, came running and the gardener's Airedale started to howl and Violet Smith, the housekeeper, had a sinking spell. One of Violet Smith's sinking spells was as memorable as the *Titanic*'s.

"Violet Smith says we eat too much meat, so it's fish again tonight." That ought to do it. He hated fish. "Marco?"

Neither the threat of screams nor fish disturbed the rhythm of his breathing.

Gilly waited. It was hot and she would have liked to sit outside on the patio for a little while to catch the breeze that started blowing in from the ocean nearly every afternoon at this time. But the patio belonged entirely to Marco. Though she was the one who'd had it designed and built, she didn't feel at ease there. She blamed it on the plants. They were all over the place, growing in stone urns and redwood boxes on the deck, and hanging from the rafters in terra-cotta pots and moss pouches held together by wire and baskets of sea grass and palm fibers.

Marco could maneuver his wheelchair among them quite easily, but Gilly was always bumping her shins on tubs of fuchsias and getting her hair caught in the tentacles of the spider plant. Marco's patio was comfortable only for people in wheelchairs, or children or dwarfs. Full-grown upright people found it hazardous. Marco's nurse, Reed, cursed when he was ambushed by the hidden barbs of the asparagus fern or the vicious spikes of the windmill palm, and even Violet Smith, who never swore, used a borderline phrase when she stepped into the lily pond while trying to avoid the soft seductive ruffles of the polypody.

For dwarfs, for children, for cripples like himself, Marco's patio was a place of fun where grownups could be booby-trapped and ordinary people made to look foolish and awkward. No child

4

ever saw it, of course. No dwarf, either. Just Gilly and Reed and Violet Smith and occasionally the doctor, who didn't say or do much because there wasn't much to say or do once he'd taught Gilly how to give injections. (She had practiced on oranges until it became quite natural for her to plunge the needle into something both soft and resistant. "As the Lord is my Savior," Violet Smith said, "that is a silly thing to do, wasting valuable oranges when you could just as easy practice on yourself." "Shut up or I'll practice on you," Gilly said.)

The sliding glass door to the patio was open and there were little rustles and stirrings among the plants as if they were whispering among themselves. They might have been fussing about the smell of fish drifting across the lawn from the kitchen. They were Marco's plants, maybe they didn't like fish any more than he did and their protests were as weak and difficult to understand as his. Not that protests would have done much good: Violet Smith had recently joined the Holy Sabbathians and each week she seemed to acquire a new conviction. This week it was fish.

"She'll be here with your dinner in a few minutes, Marco."

His rate of respiration had increased and she knew for sure now that he was awake and simply didn't want to be bothered either with food or with her.

"If you don't like it, I'll bring you something else after Violet Smith leaves for her meeting. Are you hungry?"

One side of his mouth moved and a noise came out. It didn't sound like an animal or even like one of the plants outside on the patio. It was a vegetable sound coming from a vegetable. "He's a sorrowful figure," Violet Smith often said in Marco's presence as if the stroke that had paralyzed his vocal cords and most of his body had also deafened him. This wasn't true. He had, as Gilly was well aware, ears like a fox. She and Reed had to be very cautious and time their meetings according to Marco's pills and injections.

"How would you like to eat in your Ferrari tonight?" Gilly always referred to the wheelchair as some kind of sports car. It was intended partly to amuse him and partly to soften, for her, the constant and imposing reality of it. Reed supplied her with names, most of which were unfamiliar to her—Maserati, Lotus Europa, Aston Martin, Lamborghini, Jensen-Healey.

He opened his right eye slowly and with difficulty, as if the lid had been glued shut during his afternoon sleep. It was impossible to tell from the eye's expression whether he was amused or not. Probably not. It was a very small joke and he was a very sick man. But Gilly could not help trying. Trying was part of her nature, just as giving up was part of Marco's. He had given up long before the stroke. It was merely a punctuation mark, a period at the end of a sentence.

"Okay, so it's the Ferrari. The Lamborghini's in the garage, anyway, having a tune-up . . . Eat a little fish to keep your strength up . . . Do you have to go to the john?"

The fingers of his right hand dismissed the idea.

"The doctor thinks you should drink more water if you can."

He couldn't. He wouldn't. He had given up. His hunger was only for pills, his thirst only for the fluid in the hypodermic needle.

Violet Smith came into the room with the tray, using her bony butt to close the door behind her. She was a tall, light-skinned Indian from South Dakota, Oklahoma, Michigan, Arizona, depending on her mood and whichever state happened to be in the headlines at the time. A severe tornado in Oklahoma was likely to elicit stories of a childhood spent in constant danger darting from storm cellar to storm cellar. At these times her dull brown eyes would start gleaming like polished bronze and her smooth solemn face would crack up with excitement. She forgot all about the forms she'd filled out at the employment agency which had sent her out to Gilly less than a year ago. The information was simple: Violet Smith, now forty-two, had been born and raised, educated and employed, in Los Angeles. Gilly suspected that she'd never been east of Disneyland or north of right where she was now, Santa Felicia.

"I bought this red snapper out on the wharf this morning, fresh caught." Violet Smith held the silver-lidded tray in front of her like a shield, half proudly, half defensively. "We should eat what the Lord provides for us in His seas and rivers instead of deliberately raising a bunch of cows and pigs and then slaughtering them."

"Don't proselytize," Gilly said.

"I can't do it if I don't know what it means."

"The hell you can't."

"Was I doing that what she said, Mr. Decker? Was I? . . . No?

6

No. Mr. Decker says I wasn't doing it. He shows good judgment. What a pity he can't read. It diminishes a man not to be able to read his Bible."

"He doesn't own one."

"It's not too late. He could be saved in the nick of time like I was, Jesus be praised."

"Just put the tray down and shut up."

"I think he could be saved."

"All right, work on it tonight at church. But kindly don't use our real name. I won't have a bunch of lunatics raving and ranting in public about us needing to be saved for committing God knows what sins. People might think this is a house full of thieves, crooks, murderers."

"We are all flawed," Violet Smith said coldly. "Just look who's prosetizing now."

"Proselytizing. And that's not what it means."

"Meaning is in the eye of the beholder. I think you were doing what you thought I was doing. Isn't that right, Mr. Decker? Yes? He says yes."

"Hurry up, you'll be late for your meeting."

Gilly looked at her wristwatch, noting with surprise how thin and wrinkled her arms were getting, as if her body were shrinking and aging in sympathy with Marco's no matter how much food she ate or how many times Reed assured her she was still young. "You don't look a day over forty," Reed would say. "That's because I'm not a day over forty, I'm ten years over forty." "Oh, can that crap. Who counts, anyway?" She counted. He counted. Everybody counted, whether they admitted it or not. Age was the second thing a child learned. What's your name, little girl? How old are you? . . . Gilda Grace Decker. I'm fifty.

Violet Smith put the tray on the adjustable metal table beside Marco's chair and cranked the table to the correct height. "I forgot to give you Mr. Smedler's message. He said eleven o'clock tomorrow morning in his office will be okay."

"Thanks."

"Some of these lawyers' secretaries can be very snippy."

"Yes, they can. Good night, Violet Smith."

"Good night, Mrs. Decker. And you too, Mr. Decker. I'll be praying for you both."

Gilly waited until the door closed behind her. Then she said to Marco, trying to sound quite casual, "It's nothing for you to worry about, dear. I have to talk to Smedler about stocks, bonds, trusts, that sort of thing. Very dull, lawyerish stuff."

It wasn't dull, it wasn't lawyerish, but this was not the time to tell her husband. He had to be told gradually and gently so he would understand that it wasn't just a whim on her part. She had been thinking about it, no, planning it, for several months now. Each day it seemed more and more the right thing to do until now it was more than right. It was inevitable.

Two

The wind had come up during the night, a santa ana that brought with it sand and dust from the desert on the other side of the mountain. By midmorning the city was stalled as if by a blizzard. People huddled in doorways shielding their faces with scarfs and handkerchiefs. Cars were abandoned in parking lots, and here and there news racks had overturned and broken and their contents were blowing down the street, rising and falling like battered white birds.

Smedler's office was in a narrow three-story building in the center of the city a block from the courthouse. The lesser members of the firm shared the two bottom floors. Smedler, who owned the building, kept the third floor for himself. After an earthquake a few years ago he'd remodeled it so that the only inside access to his office was by a grille-fronted elevator. The arrangement gave Smedler a great deal of privacy and power, since the circuit breaker that controlled the electric current was beside his desk. If an overwrought or otherwise undesirable client was on the way up, Smedler could, by the mere thrust of a handle, cut off the electricity and allow the client time to acquire new insights on the situation while trapped between floors.

Gilly knew nothing about the circuit breaker but she had a morbid fear of elevators, which seemed to her like little prisons going up and down. Instead she used the outside entrance, a very steep narrow staircase installed as a fire escape to appease the building-code inspector. The door at the top was locked and Gilly had to wait for Smedler's secretary, Charity Nelson, to open it.

Charity made much the same use of the bolt as Smedler did of the current breaker. "Who's there?"

"Mrs. Decker."

"Who?"

"Decker. *Decker.*"

"What do you want?"

"I have an appointment with Mr. Smedler at eleven o'clock."

"Why didn't you use the elevator?"

"I don't like elevators."

"Well, I don't like taxes but I pay them."

Charity unlocked the door. She was a short wiry woman past sixty with thick gray eyebrows so lively compared to the rest of her face that they seemed controlled by some outside force. She wore a pumpkin-colored wig, not for the purpose of fooling anyone—she frequently removed it if her scalp itched or if the weather turned warm or if she was especially busy—but because orange was her favorite color. She had been with Smedler for thirty years through five marriages, two of her own, three of his.

"Really, Mrs. Decker, I wish you'd use the elevator like everyone else. It would save me getting up from my desk, walking all the way across the room to unlock the door and then walking all the way back to my desk."

"Sorry I inconvenienced you."

"It's such a lovely little elevator and it would save you all that huffing and puffing. I bet you're a heavy smoker, aren't you?"

"I don't smoke."

"Just out of shape, eh? You should try jogging."

"Karate appeals to me more at the moment," Gilly said.

She wondered why so many employees these days acted as though they worked for the government and were not obliged to show respect to anyone. Charity's general attitude indicated that she was in the pay of the IRS, CIA and FBI and possibly God, in addition to Smedler, Downs, Castleberg, MacFee and Powell.

"Smedler's waiting for you in his office." Charity pressed a buzzer. "And Aragon will be up in a few minutes."

"Who's Aragon?"

"He's your boy. You did specify a bilingual. *N'est-ce pas?*"

"*N'est-ce pas.* In a private, personal call to Mr. Smedler."

"All of Smedler's calls go through me. I am his confidential secretary."

"You're also a smart-ass. *N'est-ce pas?*"

Charity's bushy eyebrows scurried up into her wig and hid for a moment under the orange curls like startled mice. When they reappeared they looked smaller, as if stunted by the experience. "Crude."

"Effective, though."

"We'll see."

Gilly went into Smedler's office. He rose from behind his desk and came to greet her, a tall handsome man in his late fifties. He had known Gilly for thirteen years, since the day she married B. J. Lockwood. An old school chum of B. J.'s, Smedler had been an usher at both of his weddings. He could barely recall the first—to a socialite named Ethel—but he often thought of the second with a considerable degree of amazement. Gilly wasn't young or especially pretty, but on that day, in her long white lace gown and veil, she'd looked radiant. She was madly in love. B. J. was short and fat and freckled and nobody had ever taken him seriously before. Yet there was Gilly, well over thirty and certainly old enough to know better, iridescing like a hummingbird whenever she looked at him. Smedler decided later that her appearance was, had to be, simply a matter of make-up, a dash of pink here, a silver gleam there, French drops to intensify the blue of her eyes. (He was frequently heard to remark during the next dozen years that it was not politics which made strange bedfellows, it was marriage.)

Except for an occasional business meeting or football game, Smedler saw very little of Gilly and B. J. after the marriage. The divorce eight years ago had been handled by an out-of-town firm, and the only inside story on it had come to Smedler from Charity: B. J. had run away with a young girl. Gilly was rumored to have taken the divorce very hard, though not all the effects were on the bad side. B. J., evidently suffering from guilt as well as his usual poor business judgment, had been very generous in dividing the community property.

"Sit down, my dear, sit down. Here, you'll be more comfortable in the striped chair."

He told her she looked lovely (false), that her beige silk and linen suit was very chic (true) and that he was happy to see her (a little of both).

He was, in fact, more puzzled than either happy or unhappy. Her phone call the day before had provided few details: she wanted to hire a young man who could speak Spanish and was trustworthy, to do a job for her, probably in Mexico. Why *probably?* Smedler wondered. And what kind of job? She had no business interests south of the border or even outside the country, except for a small money-hungry gold mine in northern Canada. But he had been a lawyer too long to go directly to the point.

"And how is Mr. Decker?"

"The same."

"There is still no hope?"

"Well, my housekeeper prayed for him last night at church. That's something, I suppose, when you're as hard up for hope as I am."

It had been three months or so since Smedler had seen her and she had aged considerably in such a short time. The results weren't all negative, though. There seemed to be a new strength in her face and more assurance in her manner. She'd also lost quite a lot of weight. Smedler had always admired her sense of style—no matter what costume she wore, it was difficult to imagine it suiting anyone else—and the weight loss emphasized her individuality.

"About your call yesterday," Smedler said. "It was rather enigmatic."

"It was meant to be, in case anyone was listening in on my phone or yours."

"Don't worry about mine. I have no secrets from Charity."

"I have."

"She's very discreet."

"As my housekeeper would say, discretion is in the eye of the beholder."

"Yes. Well."

"Tell me about the young man."

"His name's Aragon. Tom Aragon. He's twenty-five, bright, personable, speaks Spanish like a native, graduated from law school last spring. I find him a bit pedantic, though that could be simply his manner with me, since I'm the boss. Technically, anyway."

"How much do I pay him?"

"That depends entirely on what you want him to do. We estimate the time of a recent graduate to be worth so much an hour."

"Paying by the hour would be too complicated in this case. I'll need his total services for—well, two or three weeks, perhaps longer. What's Aragon's monthly salary?"

"I don't know for sure. Let's call Charity and—"

"No. Negative no."

"I think you may be doing Charity an injustice."

"More likely I'm doing her a justice," Gilly said. "Suppose I pay your office the amount of his salary plus a commission for the use of his services. Then I'll make separate financial arrangements with Aragon. They'll be strictly between him and me."

"Why all the secrecy, my dear?"

"If I told you anything further, you'd try and talk me out of it."

"Perhaps not. Give me a chance."

"No."

They stared at each other for a minute in silence, not hostile, but not friendly either. Then Smedler, sighing, got up and walked over to the main window. Clouds were parading across the sky like a procession of spaceships. On the earthbound street below, traffic remained sparse and sluggish. Smedler didn't look either up or down. *This is a damn stubborn woman. Okay, I can be a damn stubborn man.*

"You were B. J.'s friend," Gilly said. "But you always had a pretty low opinion of him. You treated him like a nice jolly little fellow without a brain in his head."

"Now what in hell— I mean, what brought that on? What's it got to do with anything? Even if it were true, which it isn't—"

"Oh, it's true. You made it quite obvious and it hurt. I guess it hurt me worse than it did B. J. because he never had any more faith in himself and his ability than you did. I *did*. I was *full* of faith."

"Dammit, Gilly. Get to the point."

"It's simple. If I told you what I want Aragon to do, you'd just call me a fool."

"Try me."

"No."

"Negative no?"

She didn't answer.

"By God," Smedler said. "I need a drink."

Tom Aragon closed the iron-grilled elevator door behind him and approached Charity's desk. He was a tall thin young man with horn-rimmed glasses that gave him a look of continual surprise. He'd come to Smedler's firm straight out of law school, so most of the time he was in fact surprised. The jobs assigned to him so far didn't often involve the third floor or the woman who ran it. There was a rumor, though, that she had a sense of humor if it could be found and excavated.

She must have heard the elevator door clank open and shut, but Charity didn't look up from the papers on her desk or indicate in any way that she was aware of someone else in the room.

"Hey," Aragon said. "Remember me?"

She raised her head. "Ah so. The new boy from the bottom of the bottom floor. Rather cute. Well, don't try any of the cutes on me. What do you want?"

"The boss said you'd clue me in."

"On the world in general or did you have something specific in mind?"

"This Mrs. Decker, what's she like?"

"You'd better not ask *my* opinion. She just called me a smart-ass. What do you think of that?"

"I think that's a leading question which in a court of law I wouldn't be required to answer."

"This isn't a court of law. It's a nice cozy little office with only two people in it, and one of them just asked a question and the other is going to answer."

"Very well. Mrs. Decker could be right. You and I haven't been acquainted long enough for me to judge."

Charity pushed aside her wig and scratched the lobe of her left ear in a contemplative way. "The junior members of this firm, especially the junior juniors, are usually careful to show me some respect, even a little hard homage around Christmas."

"Christmas is a long way off. Maybe I'll work up to it by then."

"I hope so."

"Now back to Mrs. Decker."

"Gilda. Gilda Grace Lockwood Decker. Lockwood was her first husband, a funny little man, looked like a drunken cherub even when he was cold sober. She married him for his money, of course, though Smedler doesn't think so. Smedler's an incurable romantic, considering the business he's in and the number of marriages he's had. Anyway, Lockwood's long gone . . . Gilly did a lot of traveling after her divorce and there was talk of various affairs in different parts of the world. Nothing really serious until she met this guy Marco Decker in Paris. Then it was clang clang, wedding bells again. She wired Smedler to send her money c/o American Express for her trousseau. Some trousseau. She must have bought half the nightgowns and perfume in France. I guess it was too much for poor old Decker. He had a stroke while they were honeymooning at Saint-Tropez. So there was Gilly, stuck with a paralyzed bridegroom in the midst of all those lovely naked young Frenchmen."

"Why were the Frenchmen naked?"

"My dear boy, it was Saint-Tropez. That's why people visit there, to see other people naked."

"It seems like a long way to go to see somebody naked."

"Well, of course only the 'in' people go to Saint-Tropez. The 'out' people like you and me, we just take off our clothes and stand in front of a mirror . . . Well, that's the sad story of Gilly. She brought Decker home, installed a lot of expensive equipment so she could keep him there and hired a male nurse to help look after him. Et cetera."

"What's included in the et cetera?"

"You can bet your life she's not wasting all those Paris nightgowns. Any more questions?"

"One," Aragon said.

"Okay, shoot."

"What joker gave you the name Charity?"

Three

The swimming pool in the middle of the patio was larger than the one at the YMCA where Aragon had learned to swim as a boy. At the bottom lay a ceramic mermaid which no YMCA would have tolerated. She wore nothing but a smirk.

A dark-haired good-looking man in very brief tight swim trunks was cleaning the pool with a vacuum. His movements were tense and angry. He pushed the vacuum back and forth across the mermaid's face as though trying to obliterate her smirk. At the same time he was conducting a monologue which Aragon assumed was aimed at him.

"Nobody manages this place. It's simply not *managed*. Take a look around, just look. Disgusting."

Aragon looked. The early-morning wind from the desert had thrown a film of dust across the water and littered it with pine needles and the petals of roses and jacarandas and cypress twigs and eucalyptus pods, all the leaves and loves and leavings of plants.

"We have two daily gardeners, a cleaning woman, a day maid, a pool boy who comes twice a week and a handyman living over the garage. So what happens? The handyman has arthritis, the gardeners say it's not their job, the day maid and cleaning woman can't be trusted with anything more complicated than a broom, and the pool boy has a term paper in biology due this week. Guess who's left? Reed. Good old Reed. That's me."

"Hello, good old Reed."

"Who are you?"

"Tom Aragon. I have an appointment with Mrs. Decker."

"Aragon. There was a fighter named Aragon once. Remember him?"

"No."

"Too young, eh? Actually, so am I. My mother told me about him. She was a fight fan. I'll never forget her actually, really—can you beat it?—putting on the gloves with me when I was six or seven years old. She was one weird old lady."

He thrust the vacuum across the mermaid's face again, then suddenly dropped it in the pool and continued his monologue. "It's only the middle of October. How could the kid have a term paper due the second week of school? And the handyman with his arthritis—hell, I'm a registered nurse, I know an arthritis case when I see it. There are over eighty different kinds and he hasn't got any of them. What he's got is a hangover, same as he had yesterday and the day before and last month and last year. If this place were *managed,* he'd be kicked out. What's behind the whole thing is this —I'm the one who uses the pool most, so if I want it clean I better bloody well clean it myself."

He was beginning to sound like a querulous old man. Aragon guessed that he was no more than thirty-five. He also guessed that Reed's bad mood hadn't much connection with merely cleaning the pool. Reed confirmed this indirectly: "Gilly told me to stick around till you got here. I had to give up my five o'clock cooking class. I was going to do beef Wellington with spinach soufflé orientale. The food around here is vile. If you're invited for dinner, split fast. Gilly hired this crazy cook who keeps getting hyped on various diets. We haven't been served any decent red meat for a week . . . I don't know what Gilly expects me to do, size you up, maybe. She can be so *obscure.*"

"Well, size me up."

Reed stared. He had green murky eyes like dirty little ponds. "You look okay."

"Thanks."

"Of course, it 's hard to tell nowadays. I had my wallet lifted last Thursday by two of the most innocent-faced chicks you ever saw . . . Go right across the patio to the glass door and shake the wind chimes good and hard. She's in Marco's room. If I hurry, maybe I can catch at least the soufflé part of my class."

"Good luck."

"A soufflé is more a matter of correct temperature and timing than luck. Do you cook?"

"Peanut butter sandwiches."

"You might *enjoy* the food around here," Reed said and disappeared around the side of the house.

It wasn't necessary for Aragon to shake the wind chimes. Gilly was waiting for him inside the door of what seemed to be a family recreation room. Its focus was a round barbecue pit level with the floor and made of used brick. The steel grill in the pit was spotless, and underneath it there were no ashes from yesterday's fire and no charcoal for tomorrow's. Only a few stains indicated the pit had been used. Above it was a huge copper hood which reflected everything in the room distorted in various degrees, much like the convex mirrors utilized in stores to spot shoplifters.

Aragon saw himself in the copper hood, a bit taller and thinner and a great deal more mysterious than he looked in the mirror of the men's room at the office. The lenses of his horn-rimmed glasses seemed almost opaque, as though they'd been designed to disguise his appearance rather than to improve his vision. He might have been a college professor who did a little spying on the side, or a spy who taught a few classes as a cover.

Gilly, too, looked different. Instead of the beige suit she'd worn earlier she had on a pink cotton dress a couple of sizes too large and espadrilles with frayed rope soles. Only the faintest coating of make-up remained on her face. The rest had disappeared, the mascara blinked off, the blushes rubbed off, the lipstick smiled or talked off. Or perhaps it had all simply been washed away in a deluge of tears. She was carrying a large manila envelope with some letters hand-printed across the front in black ink.

"Your name's Tom, isn't it?"

"Yes."

"I suppose you're curious about why I dragged you all the way out here."

"It's not far."

"Now, that's a nice evasive response. You should make a fine lawyer."

"Well, okay. I *am* curious."

"I couldn't talk to you freely this morning because I didn't want Smedler or that witch in his office to overhear." A smile swept across her face like a summer storm, leaving it refreshed, softer. "The old devil has the place bugged, you know. What did he tell you about me?"

"Very little." *Go along with her,* Smedler had said. *I'm sure she won't ask you to do anything too indiscreet. And whatever it is, you'll get some money and some experience out of it and we hang on to her business. She's one of our golden oldies.* "I don't think he has his office bugged, by the way."

"No? Why not?"

"It wouldn't be ethical."

"Tell that to Smedler sometime when I'm around. I'd love to watch his face come unglued." She put the manila envelope on a leather-topped table. Then she sat down in one of the four matching chairs and motioned for him to sit opposite her. "I've played a lot of games at this table, bridge, Scrabble, backgammon, Monopoly. This one will be new."

"What's the name of it?"

"See for yourself." She turned the manila envelope so he could read the letters. printed on the front: B. J. PHOTOGRAPHS. CERTIFICATES, ET CETERA. "Let's just call it B. J., for short."

"And the rules?"

"We make them up as we go along . . . Did Smedler tell you about B. J.?"

"No."

"Did anyone?"

"Charity mentioned him."

"I have to watch you, you really *are* evasive. What did she say?"

"That he was your first husband, B. J. Lockwood, and that he was long gone."

"Long gone. Yes, he's long gone," she repeated, almost as if she were tasting the words to identify their flavor. Spinach soufflé? Peanut butter sandwiches? Sour grapes? It was impossible for an observer to judge from her expression. "Eight years, to be precise. We'd been married five years and things were going along fine. Maybe not storybook peachy keen—we weren't kids, he'd been married before and I'd been around here and there—but certainly a whole lot better than average. At least, I thought so."

"What changed your mind?"

"He did. He took off with one of the servants, a Mexican girl no more than fifteen years old. She was pregnant. B. J. always wanted a child and I refused for a number of reasons. His family had a history of diabetes and frankly my side of it wasn't too hot either. Besides, you don't start having kids when you're in your late thirties, not unless your maternal instincts are a hell of a lot stronger than mine."

"What was the girl's name?"

"Tula Lopez. Whether B. J. was the father of her child or not, she persuaded him he was and he did the honorable thing. B. J. always did honorable things, impulsive, stupid, absurd, but honorable. So off the two of them rode into the sunset. It was what they rode in that burns me up—the brand-new motor home I'd just bought for us to go on a vacation to British Columbia. I was crazy about that thing. Dreamboat, I called it. On the first night it was delivered here to the house B. J. and I actually slept in it, and the next morning I made our breakfast in the little kitchen, orange juice and Grapenuts. A week later it was goodbye Dreamboat, B. J., Tula and the rest of the box of Grapenuts."

"What do you want me to do, get back the rest of the Grapenuts?"

She didn't smile. She merely looked pensive as if she was seriously considering the proposition. "It's hard for me to make you understand the position I'm in. How can you?—You're young, you have choices ahead of you, alternatives. Nothing's final. You get sick, you get well again. You lose a job or a girl, okay, you find another job, another girl. Right?"

"In a general way, yes."

"Well, I'm fifty. That's not very old, of course, but it cuts down on your alternatives, narrows your choices. There are more goodbyes and not so many hellos. Too many of the goodbyes are final. And the hellos—well, they've become more and more casual ... I've lost one husband and I'm about to lose another. I'm depressed, scared, sitting in that room with Marco, listening to his breathing and waiting for it to stop. When it does stop, I'll be alone. Alone, period. I have no relatives and no friends I haven't bought."

"I'm sorry."

"Good. It will help motivate you."

"To do what?"

She ran her fingers across the letters on the manila envelope as if it had turned into a ouija board and she were receiving a message. "I'd like to see B. J. again. I think— I have this strong feeling he'd like to see me, too."

"And my job is to go looking for him?"

"Yes."

"You don't even know if he's still alive."

"No."

"Or whether he'd want to contact you if he is alive."

"No."

"He and the girl, Tula, may in fact be living happily ever after with half a dozen kids."

"No." She moved her head back and forth, slowly, as if her neck had suddenly become stiff. "They only had one, a boy. He was born crippled."

"Where did you hear that?"

"B. J. wrote me a letter five years ago."

"Do you still have it?"

"It's in here."

She opened the envelope and shook out the contents on the table, snapshots, photographs, newspaper clippings, notarized documents, a bunch of letters tied together, a single one by itself.

The largest photograph was that of a bride and groom: Gilly, in a white lace gown and veil, carrying a tiny bouquet of lilies of the valley. Her expression was mischievous and girlish, as if the photographer had caught her between giggles. B. J., in morning coat and striped trousers, seemed to be sharing the joke and trying hard to keep from laughing. He had a small round face, very red, as though the strain of suppressing his laughter had sent the blood rushing to his head and the tight collar had trapped it there. He looked like a kind man who wished other people well and expected nothing but kindness from them in return. Aragon wondered how often he'd been surprised.

Gilly stared at the photograph for a long time. "We were very happy."

"I can see you were."

"Naturally he won't look like that any more. The picture was taken thirteen years ago when he was forty-one. Maybe we've both changed so much we wouldn't even recognize each other."

"You haven't changed much—some loss of weight, hair not so brown, laugh lines a little deeper."

"Those aren't laugh lines, Aragon, they're cry lines. And they're deeper, all right. They're etched all the way through to the back of my head . . . Well, anyway, I wanted to show you a picture of him as he was in his prime. I thought he was simply beautiful. I see now, of course, that he wasn't. In the cold light of an eight-year separation he may even look a little silly, don't you think?"

"No."

"No, neither do I, really." The pitch of her voice altered like an instrument suddenly gone flat. "I was crazy about him. I'm not the kind of woman who attracts men without any effort. I'm not pretty enough or tactful enough or whatever enough. I had to fight like hell to land B. J. He was married when I met him. So was Marco. I often wonder if it isn't some kind of retribution that I should lose them both."

"I don't believe in retribution."

"You haven't met Violet Smith." She put the wedding portrait back in the manila envelope, her hands trembling slightly. "You'll need some pictures of him with you when you go."

"Exactly where and when am I going?"

"When is as soon as you can get ready and we can agree on terms. Where I'm not sure . . . There are several good snapshots of B. J. Here's the last one. I took it myself. And I know it's the last because by the time the negative was developed and returned to me, B. J. was gone."

The snapshot showed B. J. behind the wheel of an elaborate new motor home. The fancy gold script across the door identified it as Dreamboat.

B. J. needed no identification. He hadn't changed much in the five years since the wedding portrait was taken. His face was still plump and ruddy, and he wore a placid smile as if nothing whatever was bothering him, least of all the fact that he was about to run away with a pregnant fifteen-year-old girl. Obviously B. J. was expecting pleasant things ahead. He may have been imagining himself in the new role of father, helping his son learn to walk, taking him to parks and zoos, teaching him to play ball, swim, sail a boat, telling him about the birds and the bees and how a little sister would be arriving, or a little brother ... *They didn't live happily ever after with half a dozen kids. They only had one, a boy. He was born crippled.*

Aragon said, "Do you have a picture of the girl, Tula Lopez?"

"Why should I? She was a servant, not a member of the family. In fact, she was only employed here for about six months. She proved incompetent and lazy. But she must have been a fast worker in her off hours. By the time I decided to fire her, the decision had been made for me."

"How did you hire her in the first place?"

"Stupidly. There was a sob story in the local newspaper about some illegal aliens who were going to be sent back to Mexico if they weren't sponsored and given jobs. B. J. and I offered to help. He had a soft heart and I had a soft head, or maybe it was vice versa. Anyhow, for a couple of softies we did some pretty hard damage." She added cryptically, "The whole thing was like a war—nobody won."

Aragon set aside the pictures he wanted to take with him: the one of B. J. in Dreamboat, another of him sitting on the edge of the pool with his feet dangling in the water, a couple of full-face Polaroid shots and a copy of his passport photo. In all of them, even the passport, he looked pretty much the same, rather homely in a pleasant way, the kind of man who posed no threat to anyone and offered no challenge. Only a woman Gilly's age could have considered him beautiful; a fifteen-year-old would see him more clearly.

Gilly picked up the letter that was separate from the others and handed it to Aragon. It was heavy. The envelope—addressed to G. G. Lockwood, 1020 Robinhood Road, Santa Felicia, California—was expensive bond paper, engraved *Jenlock Haciendas, Bahía de Ballenas, Baja California Sur.* The grade of paper and the engraving were obviously meant to impress, but the handwriting inside ruined the effect. It was like that of a child not accustomed to the use of pen and ink or the discipline of forming letters.

Aragon said, "Are you sure this is B. J.'s handwriting?"

"Pretty sure. He never learned to write decently and he forgot to take along his typewriter." She smiled wryly. "I guess it's one of the things you tend to overlook under the circumstances . . . Can you make it out?"

"I think so."

"Read it aloud."

"Why?"

"I'd like to hear how it sounds coming from a stranger. Maybe it'll give me a few laughs."

"If it's very personal, you might want to reconsider your decision."

"There are no torrid passages, if that's what's worrying you."

"I'm not worried exactly. I'd simply like to spare you any embarrassment."

"Is that what they teach you in law school, not to *embarrass* people? Don't be such a stuffed shirt."

"Smedler, Downs, Castleberg, McFee and Powell," Aragon said, "only hire stuffed shirts."

"Really?"

"To protect their image."

"Well, I don't give a cow chip about their image. And you won't either when you find out what it is."

He already had and already didn't, but he wasn't eager to admit it, especially to one of Smedler's golden oldies.

"Why are you staring at me?" she said, frowning. "Haven't you ever heard the word 'cow chip' before?"

"Sure. About every half-hour from my old man, only he said *caca de toro.* Otherwise my old lady wouldn't have understood. She never learned English."

"Where do you come from?"

"Here. I was born in the barrio on lower Estero Street."

"What's a barrio?"

"A Mexican ghetto."

"Good. You'll be able to deal with these people on their own level."

"And what level are *these people* on, Mrs. Decker?"

24

"Oh hell, don't get fussed up over some silly little remark. The Tula Lopez incident gave me kind of a prejudiced view of her whole race."

"I'll try to correct that," Aragon said. "I think we'll get along fine."

"What makes you think so?"

"I'm being paid to think so."

"Why, that's downright cynical. Did you learn such stuff in your boy scout manual? That's what Smedler called you, you know, a real boy scout."

"It's an improvement over some of the things I've called him. In private, of course, like between you and me."

"I see. The lawyer-client relationship works both ways."

"Ideally, yes."

"Smedler also told me you were a very nice young man. That worried me because I'm not a very nice old lady. I wonder if we'll have any common ground. Do you have a sense of humor?"

"Sometimes."

"Well, read B. J.'s letter and let's have a few laughs. Or didn't you believe that about me getting some laughs out of it?"

"No."

"You could be wrong. Laughter, as Violet Smith says, is in the eye of the beholder. Maybe this time I'll behold it funny. Go ahead, read it."

Four

"Dear Gilly:

"You're probably surprised to be hearing from me after all this time. I'd like to think you're even a little bit pleased too, but how could you be after the crazy way I ran out on you like that. Honestly I didn't have much control over the situation. A man has to do the right thing under certain circumstances and I did it. You know Gilly I wanted to say goodbye in a civilized manner but I was just plain scared of you. I mean how you'd take it etc. And Tula kept saying hurry up, hurry up, as if the baby was going to be born any minute. (It wasn't born for 6 months, I guess she was just anxious to get away from the immigration authorities and back to her own family.)

"Anyway here I am in this place that's hard to describe. Do you remember that time we went to a football game at the college stadium with Dave Smedler and his wife (I forget which one). Suddenly somebody yelled Whales! and we all looked out over the ocean and there they were, 5 or 6 gray whales migrating through the channel just beyond the kelp beds. It was some sight, blowing and leaping in the air and submerging again. Well Gilly you'd never guess where they were headed. Here. Right here a few hundred yards from where I sit writing this letter. Bahía de Ballenas is on a lovely little bay (it means Bay of Whales) and the gray whales come down here from California to have their calves etc. I never knew this before I got here. In fact I never thought

26

of whales as doing much along that line but naturally they do. They're human just like us.

"The water in the bay is very blue, as blue as your eyes used to be, G. G. I guess they still are, why not? I keep thinking it's such a long time since I've seen you but it really hasn't been 3 years. It seems longer to me because this place is so foreign and the people live so different. I haven't caught on to the lingo or the way they can ignore dirt and bugs and things. I often think of how you used to take 3 showers a day. You certainly were a clean person."

" 'You certainly were a clean person,' " Gilly said. "I behold that funny, don't you, Aragon?"

"Yes."

"I'm a clean person with eyes as blue as the bay where a herd of whales go to copulate and calve. What a great compliment."

"I've heard worse."

She walked over to the barbecue pit and stood for a while staring down into it as if at the ashes of old forgotten fires. "I never took three showers a day. Where'd he dredge up that idea?" She turned back with a sudden explosive sound that seemed to come all the way from her bowels. "*Ethel.* By God, he got me mixed up with *Ethel.* How do you like that? He not only can't remember which of Smedler's wives went with us to the football stadium, he can't even remember which of his own wives took three showers a day."

"The letter's been in your possession for five years. It's a little late to fuss about it now."

"She's just the type to take three showers a day. And who's fussing?"

"The evidence indicates you are."

"Okay, you want to play lawyer, define your terms."

"Fussing is an unnecessary futile display of irritability that stops short of loss of temper."

"All right, I was fussing, dammit."

"Shall I go on reading?"

"Yes."

"Now G. G. don't misunderstand what I wrote. I find the people here peculiar, who wouldn't, but the place itself is simply terrific, blue water, blue skies, no rain. It's sort of a piece of California desert like Yucca Valley for instance only it's right beside the ocean like Santa Felicia. A winning combination as you can well imagine which is why I'm betting on it. I've bet my shirt if you want the truth!

"I know how businesslike and practical you are so I'll stop beating around the bush and come right out and state the purpose of this letter. Did you notice the letterhead? In case you missed the connection it has part of my name in it, the 'lock' in Jenlock is me. Me and a fellow called Jenkins (he's awfully smart, cram full of bright ideas) are in this project together. It's cost me a mint so far. But as Jenkins says Rome wasn't built in a day for 50 pesos and you have to spend money to get money. I enclose a brochure about Jenlock Haciendas. We're going to have a lot more printed when cash becomes available. Quite a few have already been mailed to interested parties."

"Where's the brochure?" Aragon said.
"I tore it up."
"Why?"
"I have a short fuse."
"So what lit it?"
"The thing was such an obvious come-on, the high-flown descriptions of a marina, a social center, a golf course, the haciendas themselves, when all they really had was a hunk of desert and a bunch of whales. I felt like going to Smedler with the brochure and asking him to investigate. Instead, I just tore it up. As I said, I have a short fuse. I'm also pretty tight with a buck."
"B. J. asked you for money?"
"Did he ever. Read on."

"I need $100,000. Actually I need more but with that much I can at least cover current expenses and some past bills which are mounting up. Please don't think I'm just *asking* for that amount of money. I'm merely offering you the opportunity to invest in what I consider a truly promising venture. Or if you prefer instead to make me a straight loan at current interest rates that would be all right too. The former suits me better personally. We would be sort of partners again. No matter which way you send it G. G. please send it, I really desperately need it.

"I hope you won't think I'm *begging* for money. (Sounded like it there for a minute didn't it?) This is a very fine investment. I consider myself lucky to be in on the ground floor so to speak. But any kind of development takes a great deal more money than a person realizes in the beginning and Jenlock Haciendas is not your average development. It has class. Once the Americans get word of it we expect to be deluged with offers—retired people sick of smog and sportsmen looking for a vacation home (the fishing is great especially from May to September) or just plain nature lovers wanting to renew their contact with wildlife. Getting the word out, that's one of the problems we need money to solve, buying up lists of names and taking out ads in newspapers and magazines, perhaps a few T.V. spots. That would stimulate plenty of action. When you answer this (either way, yes or no, *please* answer) would you send it by registered mail? The other kind may take weeks or months or forever.

"I've thought a whole lot about you and me G. G. and what happened. I did so many dumb things I'm sorry about now like taking Dreamboat. I'm truly sorry for that because I know you'd made a lot of vacation plans etc. But Tula said we wouldn't have any place to live otherwise and she was right. When we got here there were just a lot of old shacks and people were already crammed in them like sardines. I never thought human beings could live like that but here I am doing it myself. Tula's family gradually moved in with us and I'm a sardine like the rest of them. Of course that's only temporary. When Jenlock Haciendas gets into the construction phase I intend to occupy the first one finished as a combination office and dwelling. You know I've never been in business before and I'm looking forward to trying my wings. Please answer this soon G. G.

"Hopefully, with affection, with regrets,
"B. J.
"P.S. It's terribly important for me to make good on this not just for me personally but for the boy. Unless I leave him provided for Pablo is in for a hard time. He was born crippled. You were right not to want children by me. I have rotten blood . . ."

For a minute neither of them spoke. The room seemed to be silenced by the ghosts of a long-gone man, a crippled child, a dream. Then Gilly said, "He not only had rotten blood, he had rotten judgment. I didn't send him a nickel."

"Did you answer his letter?"

"No. He didn't want an answer. He wanted the *right* answer

and I wasn't prepared to give it to him. Sure, I've often felt guilty about it. After all, every cent I own was his to begin with."

"What happened to Jenlock Haciendas?"

"I don't know. Once in a while I'd look in the real-estate section of the Los Angeles *Times* and occasionally I'd buy a San Diego paper, but I never found any mention of Jenlock Haciendas or Bahía de Ballenas. That doesn't prove anything, of course. He may have gotten the money from some place else and the project is a big success. It's possible, isn't it?"

"Yes."

"So I'm hiring you to go down and see. Hell, maybe he's struck it rich and *I'll* touch *him* for a hundred thousand dollars."

"You must consider other possibilities, Mrs. Decker. He may have left there by now. Or he may be dead."

"In either case I want to know. I also want to know what's happened to the boy."

So that's it, Aragon thought, the kid. She's rich and getting old, she has no relatives and pretty soon when Decker dies she'll be alone. A kid would bring life to the house again.

She said, "He's half Mexican, sure, but he's also half B. J., which makes him sort of related to me. Doesn't it?"

"Not legally, no."

"Who cares about the law? I'm talking about *feelings.*"

"All right. Feeling-wise, he's sort of related to you. But please bear in mind that he has a mother and that Mexicans are very much family-oriented. There's also the possibility that the child may be dead, depending, among other things, on the degree of his congenital impairment. I realize that you're living under great stress right now, and people in such circumstances sometimes make plans based on an unrealistic assessment of the facts."

"You realize that, eh? Well, I realize that lawyers often like to use twenty words when one will do."

"How about two?"

"All right."

"Cool it."

"What does that mean exactly?"

"Even if I find the kid he won't be for sale."

She looked almost stunned for a moment. "Perhaps we should go back to the twenty-word system."

"It has certain advantages."

"Your style takes a little getting used to, Aragon, but then, so does mine. We might be able to work together satisfactorily. What do you think?"

"I don't pick the clients," Aragon said. "They have to pick me."

"Okay., I pick you."

"Fine."

She had a check ready for him, $2,500 made out to Tomas Aragon and marked "Legal services." "This should cover your air fare, car rental, living expenses, and of course, bribes. If anyone asks you, you can say you work for the local police. They may not believe you but they'll believe the money. Are you familiar with Baja California?"

"I've been to Tijuana."

"Then the answer is no. I've done a little research on my own. You can fly down as far as Rio Seco and rent a car there. It has the last car-rental agency until the southernmost tip of Baja. Bahía de Ballenas is roughly halfway between. It's not marked on most maps. Just keep driving south until you come to it. There's a new road that goes part of the way along the coast. They call it a highway but you'd better not expect too much."

Aragon put the check in his wallet and then returned the letter from B. J. to its envelope. "Do you mind if I keep this for a while? The references might be useful."

"Take it. By the way, let's get something clear. I could hire any investigator for a job like this a lot cheaper than you're going to cost me."

"Why don't you?"

"I'm paying for discretion, for the privacy of a lawyer-client relationship. You're not to tell anyone the nature of our business, not Smedler, not the authorities, not even your wife. Do you have a wife?"

"Yes. I haven't been seeing much of her, though. She's in her first year of residency in pediatrics at a hospital in San Francisco."

"Smart, eh?"

"Yes."

"What's her name?"

"Laurie Macgregor."

"Why didn't she take your name?"

"She already had one of her own."

"All very modern and with it. I see . . . I bet she's pretty."

"I think so."

"Describe her, nonlawyer style."

"Nonlawyer style, she's a dynamite chick."

Gilly was staring pensively at her image in the copper hood of the barbecue pit. "I wonder, if I were in my twenties again, would anyone call me a dynamite chick?"

"On the evidence presented so far I would assume that you were and that you would be so designated."

"Hey, that's nice, Aragon. You and I are going to be pals. You know what else? You'll make a very good lawyer."

"Well, if I don't, I hope I'll be married to a very good pediatrician."

Aragon hadn't intended it to be funny, but she laughed as if he'd made the joke of the century. He suspected that the dynamite-chick business had left his new pal, Gilly, a little intoxicated.

Five

Violet Smith picked her way carefully around the side of the house past the thorns of the carissa and the spiked leaves of the century plants and the gopher holes in the lawn. She had seen Aragon's car parked in the driveway and had been on her way to the barbecue room in the hope of overhearing something interesting when Mr. Decker's bell rang. Reed was off duty and the day girl had already left, so it was Violet Smith's Christian obligation to answer the bell. Mr. Decker had to go to the bathroom, which was messy and took forever, so that by the time she finished cleaning up, twenty minutes or more had elapsed.

Crossing the patio, she stooped to retrieve a stray leaf caught between two flagstones. Out of the corner of her eye she could see Mrs. Decker talking to a strange man. She couldn't make out the words but they must certainly have been funny because Mrs. Decker suddenly began laughing like some giddy young girl. Violet Smith transferred the leaf to the apron pocket of her uniform and slid open the screen door.

Mrs. Decker immediately sobered up and looked her age again. "You can see I'm busy, Violet Smith."

"Mr. Decker is agitated. I think he heard a strange car come up the driveway and wants to know what is it doing here."

"It's waiting for Mr. Aragon," Gilly said brusquely.

"Do I go back and tell him?"

"No. No, I'll do it ... Aragon, please stay here for a minute while I check my husband, will you?"

"Don't hurry," Aragon said. "I have lots of time."

After she'd gone Violet Smith studied Aragon carefully and at length. "How come you have lots of time? Don't you work?"

"I'm working now."

"You give a good impression of just standing around."

"Practice, Miss Smith. Years of practice ... Mrs. Smith?"

"Violet Smith is my true name, both here and There. When people don't call me that, I pay them no mind. I figure they might be talking to someone else. There are millions of Smiths."

She had a point and Aragon guessed that she would cling to it even if it impaled her. He said, "I hope I haven't disturbed Mr. Decker."

"He's *agitated.* That could be good or bad, depending. I never know. I can't understand those monkey noises of his, meaning no disrespect. He heard a strange car and we don't get many strangers around here."

"Why not?"

"Mrs. Decker had Reed put up a lot of signs to scare people off, like No Peddlers, No Trespassing, Private Property, Beware of Dogs. We don't even have a dog, except one of the gardeners brings his Airedale along in the truck which howls. The gardeners are both long-haired heathens ... Have you been saved?"

"I think so."

"Aren't you sure?"

"It's not the sort of thing one can be sure about until—well, until later."

"If you think there's any doubt, it would be better to find out now than then."

"Yes, I guess it would."

"You know, you kind of remind me of my son. I don't see much of him any more. I never raised a hand to that boy until the day he vilified the Lord. He diminished Jesus and I had to slug him. My hand pained me for several weeks. I could hardly hold my Bible."

She began dusting the glass table with a piece of tissue which she produced from one of the half-dozen pockets of her uniform.

It was apparent from her vigorous movements that her slugging hand had been completely cured and that Violet Smith was ready for another round at the sound of the bell. She was a powerful woman with thick wrists, and shoulders as wide as Aragon's.

He said, "Why does Mrs. Decker want to scare people off?"

"They might disturb Mr. Decker. He's pretty far gone, a real sorrowful figure. I overheard Reed asking the doctor one day if it wouldn't be more humane to pull out the plugs. I couldn't understand what they were talking about until the doctor used the word, 'euthanasia.' Then I stepped right up and said I was against it. The doctor was polite enough, but oh, that Reed has a dirty tongue in his head. I felt duty-bound to report the incident to Mrs. Decker. Maybe I shouldn't have."

"Why not?"

"Wow, she threw a terrible fit, crying and carrying on and screaming how she wanted to have her plugs pulled out too. Then she drank a lot of booze. I told her, 'You can't drown your troubles, Mrs. Decker, because troubles can swim.' *Well.* If you think Reed has a dirty tongue in his head you should have heard *her.* My ears cringed. 'Sticks and stones,' I said to her, 'sticks and stones can break my bones but words will never hurt me.' She told me what I could do with every stick and stone between here and Seattle."

"It wasn't one of your more popular nights, apparently."

"Oh, I forgave her. I knew she was just scared like everybody else who won't accept Jesus. Scared of the old man dying and leaving her alone, and scared of dying herself. I'm used to her bad language, anyway. She's not a true-born lady like the first Mrs. Lockwood. Mrs. Decker was the second Mrs. Lockwood."

"You're acquainted with the first?"

"I see her at church twice a week. We often share the same hymn book. She's a soprano but not one of those screechy ones, just soft and ladylike as befits her birth."

"Is she aware that you work for Mrs. Decker?"

"Sure. At our regular evening meetings we're encouraged to stand up and talk out our predicaments and troubles. Then afterwards we all sit around and help each other."

"Or not."

"Or not," Violet Smith agreed crisply. "We aren't *geniuses,* you know. It's the feeling that counts, the realizing you're not alone, someone else cares and wants to help."

"Your church meetings sound very interesting."

"Oh, they are. They're what really converted me. I didn't mind giving up carnality, jewelry and red meat in return for comradeship and an afterlife."

"I think you made the right decision."

"You do?"

"Yes."

"You're not being sarcastic like Reed or Mrs. Decker?"

"No."

"I'm glad. You know, when you're stuck in a place like this most of the time, you've got to have something lively, something hopeful, going on outside. The death house—that's what some of the employees call it. All the pretty flowers and trees, the sun shining, the pool, the birds singing, none of it makes any difference when you're waiting for someone to die. You want to tell the birds to shut up and the sun to drop down and the flowers to fold their petals and blow away. Imagine telling a bird to shut up. But I did one day. There was this little red-headed creature singing on top of the TV antenna and I screamed at him, 'Stop it, shut up, don't you know someone's dying down here?' "

"Did you ever express these feelings at any of your church meetings?"

"No. They'd think I was a loony. ... Listen, I hear Mrs. Decker coming back. She's suspicious. Pretend I never said a word, not one word, agreed?"

"Agreed."

Gilly re-entered the room through the inside door that connected it with the main part of the house. She looked flushed, as though she'd been engaged in some strenuous physical or emotional exertion. She said, "I suppose Violet Smith has talked your ear off."

"No."

"That's peculiar. She does it to everyone else."

"Oh, I do not," Violet Smith said coldly and went outside, pushing the screen door shut behind her as hard as she could.

Gilly waited for her to disappear around the side of the house. "My husband's all right. He sometimes reacts badly when Reed goes off duty or when something unusual happens."

"And I'm an unusual happening?"

"To Marco, yes. I'd like you to meet him. He sees the same people day after day and I'm sure he'd enjoy some different company for a change. No matter what impression Violet Smith gave you, Marco can hear and often understand as well—or almost as well—as you and I can."

"It might be better for me to see him some other time."

"This is the time I want you to see him, right now. I have my reasons."

"Very well, Mrs. Decker. You're the boss."

Gilly spoke his name softly. "Marco?"

Nothing happened for a minute. Then the wheelchair, which had been facing the patio, suddenly and noiselessly turned and Aragon had his first glimpse of Marco Decker. He seemed a little smaller than life. His face was pale and shriveled, and around his head there was a fringe of sparse silky hair like a baby's. Under the lap robe his knees showed almost as thin and sharp as elbows. A mohair shawl was wrapped around his shoulders and fastened at the front with a safety pin, the extra large size used for diapers. It heightened the image of an old man returning through the maze of years to his infancy.

This was Aragon's first time in the presence of a terminally ill person and he understood more clearly what Violet Smith had been talking about. The imminence of death altered the meaning of things. The plants outside the window looked too grotesquely healthy, the hummingbirds among the fuchsia blossoms were too lively and brilliant, the warmth of the sun useless, even offensive. Aragon felt the reaction of his own body, the increased flow of adrenaline that increased his heartbeat and signaled his muscles to fight or flight. *Run away, man. Drop down, sun. Shut up, bird.*

"Marco dear, this is Tom Aragon, the young man from the lawyer's office."

"How do you do, Mr. Decker," Aragon said.

The fingers of one of Marco's hands twitched slightly in acknowledgment of the greeting.

Gilly said, "I thought I'd introduce Aragon to you and tell you exactly why I sent for him, Marco. I'd rather have kept it secret to spare you any worry, but I know you're bound to hear hints about it from Reed or Violet Smith or one of the maids, or even from me unintentionally. When very little occurs in a house, whatever does occur is repeated and blown up out of proportion. This is a small thing, actually."

Marco's right eye blinked. The movement was slow and labored but the expression in the eye itself was clear: *Hurry up, get on with it, I haven't much time.*

"I won't tell you if you're going to fuss about it because it isn't that important."

Hurry, hurry, giddyap, giddyap.

"Now, don't be upset . . . I've often talked to you about B. J., haven't I? And I've told you what happened. We have no secrets from each other. Well, I've been thinking, what if B. J. struck it rich, down in Mexico, I mean *rich* rich. Some of these developers rake in millions and millions, and while he was always a lousy businessman, maybe this time he struck it lucky. I talked to Smedler. He said I'd be a fool not to try and cash in on it if really big money is involved. He said I should make an effort to find B. J."

Aragon stared at her. There wasn't the subtlest change of expression on her face or the slightest quaver in her voice to indicate that she'd just told three lies in three sentences.

"Well, now you know what Mr. Aragon is doing here. He's collecting material on B. J. so he'll know where to look first, and so on. I showed him some pictures of B. J. and also the last letter I received from him five years ago. There now. That shouldn't upset you, should it?"

Marco's paralyzed eye remained half open but the good one was closed. He might have gone to sleep out of weariness or boredom; he might have died.

"Don't do that. Don't pretend you're sleeping when you're not, Marco, just to make me go away. I'll go away in a minute when I've finished explaining to you . . . Listen, he treated me badly, he almost destroyed me. It was a long time ago and everything ought to be forgotten and forgiven by now. But it's not. He *owes* me. I want to see him pay a few more damages."

The wheelchair turned, as it had before, without a sound and faced the patio again, the plants, the birds, the sun.

"All right, Marco, I'm leaving. I won't bother you any more."
She opened the door and went out into the corridor. With a final

glance at the man in the wheelchair, Aragon followed her. "Perhaps I shouldn't have told him but I felt I'd better. He'll be quite reasonable once he gets used to the idea. If he is or isn't, I must go ahead with the project anyway. I've been considering it a long time and I have no intention of giving it up. You think—you may think I'm doing all this out of revenge."

"I may."

"In fact you do."

"Well, I was just wondering what the going price is for a pound of flesh."

"The same as it's always been," Gilly said quietly. "A pound of flesh."

Outside, the wind had gone down and all the billowy clouds had broken up and were strung across the sky in shreds. The plastic hose of the pool vacuum was floating in the water where Reed had dropped it. It looked like a giant white sea snake coiled to strike.

Later in the evening he called his wife, Laurie, at the hospital in San Francisco. The background noises and her crisp confident voice indicated she was on ward duty. It was the professional voice she used to intimidate germs and head nurses and to calm frightened children and their parents.

"Dr. Macgregor speaking."

"Tom Aragon here. Remember him?"

"Vaguely. Describe him."

"Dark-haired, kind of funny-looking, pale, could probably use some medical attention."

"Sorry, that's not the Tom Aragon I know who happens to be very handsome, well-built, healthy, intelligent—"

"Listen, we're in the money, Laurie."

"You robbed a bank."

"No."

"Blackmailed an old lady."

"Close. One of Smedler's clients wants me to find her first husband, who's somewhere in Baja California. I'm not sure why, exactly. She's given half a dozen reasons, which is five too many. But I took the job—and her money—and I'm leaving for Rio Seco tomorrow morning."

"When was your last smallpox vaccination?"

"I don't recall."

"Better check it out. You had a tetanus booster this summer after you swam into the jellyfish, so that's okay."

"Laurie, for Pete's sake, you're not going into your mother-hen routine?"

She ignored the question. "It's no joke about the water in Mexico. Don't drink it. Don't even brush your teeth with it. Use beer."

"I never heard of brushing teeth with beer."

"You could start a trend."

"Hey, I miss you."

"Save the soft talk for later. Now, don't even look at any vegetable that's not cooked or fruit that's not peeled. *Turista* is bad enough—you can pick up some Lomotil to take care of that—but infectious hepatitis is worse, in fact it's sometimes fatal . . . I miss you, too . . . Did you know there's a place in Mexico where Hansen's disease is endemic?"

"What's Hansen's disease? On second thought—"

"Leprosy."

"Don't tell me any more or I'll quit right now and send all the money back to Mrs. Decker."

"*No.* I mean, we can use it. Just be careful. Hansen's disease isn't contagious, but pick up some halazone tablets to put in water in case of emergency. Have you any antibiotics to take with you?"

"I don't know."

"Check the medicine cabinet for tetracycline or ampicillin. Also insect repellent, especially one containing D.E.E.T. And you'd better have your hair cut very short. There'll be less chance of pediculosis."

"I hesitate to ask—"

"Head lice."

"Head lice?"

"Well, you're not going to be staying at the Ritz, you know. Now, do you think you can remember all the things I've told you?"

"Sure. Absolutely. I'm making notes."

She laughed. "You're not really, are you?"

"I would be if I happened to have a pencil and some paper and knew how to spell tetracycline and ampicillin and Lomotil . . . How's the job going?"

"Fine. Long hours, hard work, lethal food. But the kids are great. I've got one on my lap right this minute, a Vietnamese orphan. He's a very sick little boy, but as long as someone is carrying him around or holding him he's perfectly quiet. Do you suppose we'll ever have any kids, Tom?"

"Under present circumstances it seems unlikely."

"Circumstances change."

"The decision will be yours, anyway. My minimal role merits only a fraction of a vote."

"What would it be, though?"

"I'm not sure I want to take a chance on any kid inheriting my myopia or your tendency to cry at movies."

"I don't cry at movies any more."

"Why not?"

"I don't get a chance to see any. On my off-hours I sleep. I just plain sleep."

"You could never sleep plain, Laurie. You sleep very, very pretty."

"What are you trying to do, make me quit my job and come running?"

"Not on your life," he said soberly. "I may need somebody to support me."

"It'll be fun, won't it, when I hang up my shingle and you hang up your shingle."

"At least our shingles will be together. Maybe they'll have little shingles."

"Tom, you're not really beefing, are you?"

"No."

"Honestly?"

"I'm not beefing. I just happen to miss you and wish you were here or I was there and the hell with Mrs. Decker's first husband."

"I love you, too. Listen, I have to go, they're paging my number. Take care of yourself. Promise?"

"I promise to brush my teeth with beer and avoid head lice and lepers. Tell the little guy on your lap good night for me."

"I will. Good night, Tom. I think you're terribly nice."

After he hung up he sat staring at the phone as though he half expected it to ring again. No matter how often or how long he and Laurie talked to each other, the conversation always seemed unfinished. He wanted to pick up the phone and call her back, but he thought of the kids waiting for her on the ward and how tired she'd sounded under the cool professional voice and how selfish he'd be to make things tougher by leaning on her.

He went to the refrigerator and poured himself a glass of beer out of a recapped quart bottle. It was a little flat, the kind good for cleaning teeth. He swished some around in his mouth by way of practice.

Six

Once he got off the plane in Rio Seco, Aragon lapsed naturally into Spanish. It was the language of his boyhood, his family and friends, the streets where he'd played, even his school at recess and before and after classes. During classes the official language was English. *You are in the United States of America, children, and you are expected to speak the language of the United States of America.* They did, when teacher was listening. When she wasn't, the younger children said, *Qué mujer tan fea,* and the older ones, *Chinga tu madre.*

The car that he'd reserved by phone from Los Angeles was waiting for him, a compact Ford that looked older than its odometer indicated. When he checked it over, he found the oil gauge registered low, two of the tires needed air and the gas tank was only half filled. The man who seemed to be in charge at the rental agency, Zalamero, assured him that in all his years of experience in the business, almost one, such oversights had never before been detected. Zalamero spoke a mixture of Spanish and English slang sometimes called Spanglish. Aragon asked him for directions to Bahía de Ballenas.

"Bahía de Ballenas, why are you going there? It's an el dumpo."

"I'm thinking of buying some property."

"My wife's cousin has some super-duper property near here that he's willing to sell cheap, so cheap you wouldn't believe."

"That's right, I wouldn't," Aragon said. "Now, about Bahía de Ballenas."

"Okey-dokey, you drive south two hundred kilometers or so until the road turns inland. You stop. You're at a place called Viñadaco, another el dumpo, but they have tourist cabins, cafés, gas pumps. Get some gas and more water and start up again. Now you drive slow, very slow, in second gear, because the highway is going *east* and you are going *west*."

"Are there any road signs?"

"No, no, no. You ask a person. This person answers and you have a nice talk, maybe a cup of coffee, a little social life. It's much better than signs."

Aragon tried to imagine the effect of this kind of social life on the Hollywood Freeway. After the initial chaos it might be quite pleasant for those who weren't going anywhere in a hurry.

Zalamero said anxiously, "You won't tattletale the agency in the U.S. about the oil and tires?"

"No, but you should be more careful."

"Yes, yes, yes, you bet I will be. I will personally inspect every part of every car every day."

"Your social life is bound to suffer."

"You've convinced me I have a duty to my customers. Besides, I can talk while I inspect. All Zalameros can do two things at once . . . How soon will you bring the car back?"

"A week, perhaps less."

"Go with God."

"Thanks."

He paid a deposit on the Ford and a week's rental in advance. It was nearly two o'clock when he started the engine.

For about twenty kilometers beyond Rio Seco the road continued to be fairly good. Then gradually it began to deteriorate, as if the surveyors and the foreman and the key workers had lost interest and dropped out, one by one.

The traffic was heavier than Aragon had expected but still sparse: dilapidated pickups and compacts and subcompacts with Mexican license plates, and newer vehicles mostly from the Western states, vans, trucks with cabover campers and complete houses on wheels like Dreamboat. The road hadn't been built with Dreamboats or highway speeds in mind. It was narrow, the curves were poorly banked and the roadbed inadequately compacted. Drivers accustomed to American standards of engineering took the curves and unexpected dips too fast in vehicles that were too wide and heavy. The accident rate, according to a safety pamphlet distributed on the plane by an insurance company, was extremely high.

He began to understand why his rented Ford looked old for its age. Sand blew across the roadway from the low barren hills to the east and the coastal dunes to the west, pitting the car's finish and burrowing its way through the closed windows. At times it was so fine and white that it swept past like a blizzard of talcum powder. Aragon could feel it clinging to the roof of his mouth and the membranes of his nose. It scratched the inside of his eyelids and mixed with the sweat of his palms on the steering wheel to form a sticky film of clay. The cars and vans and campers heading north were suddenly all white. They passed like ghosts of accidents. A few kilometers farther, the powder turned to sand again. *If I were going in the opposite direction, I'd be halfway to San Francisco by now. Laurie might manage a couple of days off and we could splurge and stay at the Clift. Just stay. No night clubs, no theaters, no fancy dinners . . .*

He braked to avoid a jackrabbit leaping across the road. Except for an occasional gull soaring overhead, the rabbit was the only sign of wildlife he'd seen. It was an inhospitable countryside. Clumps of creosote bushes and spindly spikes of cholla were the main vegetation, with here and there some mesquite or a palo triste like a billow of gray smoke.

Just short of two hundred kilometers the landscape suddenly changed, indicating the presence of fresh water and some kind of irrigation system. Fields of beans and chili peppers alternated with groves of palm trees. An abandoned sugar mill overlooked a scattering of adobe houses with children playing outside, and chickens and goats and burros wandering loose among them. This, according to a sign on the gas pump where Aragon stopped, was the village of Viñadaco.

The gas pump was operated by an entire family. While the

man filled the tank, his wife cleaned the front windshield and a couple of small girls cleaned the back. A boy no more than five wiped off the headlights with the torn sleeve of his shirt while two teenagers lifted the hood and stared expertly at the engine without doing anything. They were mestizos, half-Indians, copper-skinned and thin-featured, with black eyes and straight black hair. Their solemn dignity reminded Aragon of Violet Smith.

He asked the woman for directions to Bahía de Ballenas.

"Nobody goes there."

"I do."

"But the road turns the other way towards the gulf. And it's late, it will soon be dark. You might get stuck in the sand or lost."

They were valid reasons but not the real one: she happened to have a vacant cabin which she rented out to tourists. Nothing fancy, of course, no running water or electricity, but a nice clean bed. For this nice clean bed the asking price was about the same as for a suite at the Beverly Hilton. The señora admitted that the price was high, but she didn't offer to change it and Aragon didn't argue. It was Gilly's money. If she wanted to come down here and haggle over it, let her. He was tired and hungry.

He ate at the nearest place, a shoebox-sized café overlooking a pond where a dozen or so coots were floating on the water and foraging on the banks. When he was a child he'd often eaten coot, which his mother called black mallard. This sounded better but didn't improve the taste or texture. As he ate the *machaca* he was served, a kind of hash, he tried to identify its contents. Coot maybe, dried goat meat probably, and chilis unmistakably, the small green innocent-looking kind that lit up his mouth and throat and brought tears to his eyes to put out the fire. Dessert was a dish of fried beans and a cactus fruit with sweet juicy pulp. He drank two bottles of beer and bought two extra to take with him in case his teeth were extra dirty.

He returned to the gas pump and the Viñadaco Hilton. The señora had left a kerosene lamp burning for him, and a basin with a pitcher of water and two small towels. After he'd stripped and washed he sat down to drink some beer. Almost immediately he discovered that the Viñadaco Hilton had one other thing which the Beverly Hilton didn't—mosquitoes. The first bite coincided with the first twinge in his stomach. He went to sleep trying to remem-

ber some of the things Laurie had urged him to take along—
antibiotics ... head lice ... tooth beer ... Laurie, I miss you ...

He woke up at dawn. So did every man, woman, child and
beast in the village. Children chanted, donkeys brayed, roosters
crowed, dogs barked. Aragon got up and opened the door. The sun
was shining and a cool moist wind was blowing steadily in from
the sea. It was the kind of day he wanted to rush out to meet.

During the night the señora's conscience must have been bothering her: she appeared at the door with a cup of coffee and two
tortillas rolled up with guava jelly and a pot of hot water.

"Are you hungry?"

"Yes."

"And you want hot water. Why do Americans always want
hot water?"

"To shave."

"You have hardly anything to shave. And who is going to see
you in *that* forsaken place? I've never been there myself but I hear
the people are very dark-skinned and ignorant."

While he shaved she gave him directions to Bahía de Ballenas
and even borrowed his pen to draw him a little map. He didn't put
much faith in the map—she held the pen as though it were the first
one she'd ever used.

Also during the night someone—probably the two teenaged
boys who were now leaning casually against the gas pump—had
washed the Ford. He appreciated the gesture, but unfortunately the
car was now parked in the middle of a large puddle of water. He
took off his shoes and socks, waded through the puddle and
climbed in behind the wheel. His feet felt pleasantly refreshed.
People checking out of the Beverly Hilton might have their cars
waiting at the front door, but they didn't get guava jelly tortillas,
farewell footbaths and all the fresh air they could breathe.

He stopped at the café where he'd eaten dinner the previous
evening and picked up a dozen bottles of beer. If the señora's
prediction came true and he was going to get lost, he might as well
do it in style. He was on a little dirt road a couple of miles south
of Viñadaco when he stopped to consult the map and discovered
that the señora had neglected to return his pen. He might ask for
it on the way back, assuming he arrived at any place to come back

from. Or, better yet, he would put it down as a business expense, Gilly's small and undoubtedly grudging contribution toward international relations. She was, in her own words, pretty tight with a buck.

The road climbed uphill along a cliff for a while, then dropped down again between sand dunes, sometimes disappearing entirely, only to reappear a few yards farther on like a magician's scarf. At one point there was a fork not indicated on the map. The east branch showed signs of more frequent use than the west. If the señora was correct in claiming that no one went to Bahía de Ballenas, then the west branch seemed the better choice. He took it.

The sun, which had seemed so gentle and friendly at dawn, was turning into a monster that couldn't be pacified or controlled. He wasn't sure at what point or why the Ford's air conditioner blew out, but he suddenly became aware that he was riding in an oven with the heat turned on full and that he'd better do something about it fast. He stopped in the meager shade of some mesquite, opened all the car windows and two of the bottles of beer. The beer had been in the oven with him and did nothing to quench his thirst, but it improved his general outlook from terrible to bad. He was, if not lost, certainly misplaced. The road, which had never been more than a series of tire tracks, was now visible only at times when the capricious wind deposited the sand short of it or beyond it. He wondered how B. J. had ever maneuvered a vehicle the size of Dreamboat as far as Bahía de Ballenas. Of course the girl, Tula, had lived in this area with her relatives and was familiar with it. She would have known which road to avoid, and this was undoubtedly it.

A mixed flock of gulls and smaller, more agile sea birds often flew low over the car like an advance patrol. They had a cool confident air as if they knew exactly what they were doing. Aragon started the engine again and followed them.

At the top of the next sand dune Bahía de Ballenas came into view, a half circle of sparkling blue water surrounded by desert. A few small fishing boats were tied up at a battered pier. The only other boat visible rode at anchor in the middle of the bay, a gray sloop sleek as a dolphin. It was flying both American and Mexican ensigns, a purple-and-white yacht-club burgee and an officers' flag. At the water's edge were some salt-water conversion tanks, an old fish cannery that looked abandoned and half a dozen wooden shacks. On higher ground stood the crumbling remains of a small adobe mission. Between the mission and the shacks was the inevitable collection of children and chickens and dogs and goats all covered with dust. An invisible and insurmountable barrier seemed to separate the clean clear water of the bay from the dirty little village and its people.

The children, ranging in age from a baby barely able to walk to a twelve- or thirteen-year-old girl, were ragged and shoeless, like the mestizos of Viñadaco, but different in appearance. These were darker-skinned, with rounded features and soft expressive brown eyes. Under their grimy clothes their bodies looked well-nourished and healthy except for one boy who had a withered left leg.

Aragon addressed the girl. "Hello."

"Hello."

"Is this place Bahía de Ballenas?"

She nodded. The other children broke into giggles as if they'd never before heard such a funny question. Was this place Bahía de Ballenas? Of course. It had to be. There wasn't any other place.

"What's your name?"

"Valeria. What's your name?"

"Tomas."

"I have a chicken named Tomas. He doesn't lay eggs and he's mean."

"Boys don't lay eggs."

"Chickens do."

"Boy chickens don't."

"*I* know *that.* I just *told* you he doesn't."

"Okay, okay. Whatever game we're playing, you win."

She accepted her victory with the equanimity of a champion. "I'm grown up. Next year I might marry my cousin Raul. He lives in a real house beyond that hill over there."

She pointed. Aragon couldn't see any house and there were half a dozen hills all exactly the same. He turned his attention to the boy with the withered leg. "What's your name?"

"Okay okay."

"Is that what they call you?"

"Okay okay."

Suddenly the boy thrust his hand in the window of the car and honked the horn. The children began running away, shrieking with laughter, followed by their squawking barking baaing retinue of animals. He got out of the car intending to follow them, but a voice stopped him, the high cracked voice of someone very old: "Good morning. Is there anything I can do for you?"

Aragon turned. A man was standing in the doorway of the crumbling mission. He wore a straw hat and the remnants of a brown priest's robe tied at the waist with a piece of rope. He was tiny and shriveled as though he'd been left too long in the sun. One of his eyes was bloodshot and dripped tears that ran down the deepest groove in his cheek. Flecks of salt from previous tears glistened on his face when he pushed back his hat.

"Are you lost, friend?"

"This is Bahía de Ballenas?"

"Yes."

"Then I'm not lost. I've been looking for it."

"Not many people look for us. This is a pleasant surprise. What is your name?"

"Tomas Aragon."

"Everyone calls me padre. I once had a real name, but it slips my mind now and then. No matter. Such things are not important where everybody knows everybody. Will you come inside where it's cool?"

"Thank you, padre."

"Padre is a courtesy title only. I have long since left the Church, but it has not left me. I am allowed to live here. The villagers and I have mutual respect. I give them comfort when I can and take it when I must."

The doorway was so low that Aragon had to stoop to enter. The man noticed his hesitation.

"Have no fear for your safety, friend. These walls will last beyond my time and yours. Adobe is a very fine building material in a climate like this. It is strong. And more, it is friendly, absorbing heat during the day and giving it back during the night."

The room was only a little larger than the cabin Aragon had occupied the previous night at Viñadaco, but it was cool and comfortable, furnished with a cot, a table and chairs and an adobe bench in front of the altar. Dwarfing the room and its contents was a life-sized and extremely ugly statue of the Virgin Mary. It was all gray like an angel of death.

50

The padre looked up at her with affection. "I made her myself. The original statue fell and broke during an earthquake, so I spent some years, ten, perhaps twelve or thirteen—*tempus fugit*—fashioning a replacement. It is the only gift I will leave behind for the villagers when I die."

"It's very impressive."

"Yes. Yes, I think so. Inside, to hold her together, I piled stones which the children helped me collect. And the sculpting material is what we use to make our cooking stoves, water poured over hot ashes and mixed into a paste. Each day, every time I had a fire, I added a little, and there she is." He crossed himself. "Now I don't have to worry so much that the villagers will lose touch with God after I'm gone. They will have the Blessed Virgin to remind them . . . I was about to eat my midday meal. Will you be my guest?"

"Thanks."

"Simple fare, a bit of mullet I cooked this morning and some pitahaya. The Americans in La Paz used to call it organ-pipe cactus, so it seems most fitting to serve it in my little church, doesn't it?"

"Yes."

"I'm sorry, I've forgotten your name. My memory has dulled with age."

"Tomas Aragon."

"Would it be suitable if I called you Tomas?"

"I'd be pleased."

The two men sat down facing each other across the wooden table. The padre blessed the piece of mullet on the battered tin plate and waved away the flies buzzing around it. Though the fish had a slight greenish iridescence, it tasted all right, and the pitahaya was similar to what he'd been served at the café in Viñadaco, only sweeter and juicier. After the meal Aragon went out to the car and brought in several bottles of beer.

"My saints and sinners," the padre said. "This is a great surprise."

"It's very warm, if you don't mind . . ."

"Oh, no no no. I like it any way at all. Tecate. I haven't tasted that for a long time. This is an occasion, Tomas, yes, a celebration. We ought to make a toast. What do you suggest?"

"To your health, padre."

"To your safe journey, Tomas."

"To your village and the future of its children."

"That's the best toast. To their future."

The two men drank. The beer was the temperature of restaurant tea.

"One of the girls has her future planned," Aragon said. "She will marry her cousin Raul and live in a real house."

"That would be Valeria. Always planning, already like a woman."

"I haven't seen any real houses in Bahía de Ballenas. Perhaps she is dreaming."

"Perhaps. Now if you will excuse me for a few minutes, I'll go and bury the remains of our meal."

"Let me help."

"No. No, it won't take long. Sit and contemplate the Blessed Virgin."

It would have been difficult in that small room to contemplate anthing else, so Aragon did as he was told. In spite of the strong beer, the statue of the Virgin remained ugly. There was a frightening determination about her face that reminded him of Violet Smith. It was now Sunday afternoon. In a few hours Violet Smith would be setting out for church to sing hymns—sharing her hymn book with B. J.'s first wife, Ethel—and stand up afterward in front of the assemblage to voice her problems and concerns. Perhaps she would tell about the young man who was hired by B. J.'s second wife to go on a confidential mission, giving names and places and dates and whatever other details she might have wormed out of Gilly or Reed, or overheard on an extension phone or through a thin closed door.

When the padre returned, his breath was wheezing in and out of his lungs like the air through an old leaky accordion.

Aragon said, "Do you teach the children?"

"Whatever and whenever possible."

"I noticed one of the boys has a deformed leg and acts retarded."

"A child of God."

"His skin seems somewhat lighter than that of the others. His parents—"

"He is an orphan."

"Where does he live?"

"In Mexico all people love children. Pablo can live anywhere."

"But where *does* he live?"

"It would break hearts if he were ever taken away. If you have any such thought, any reason—"

"No. None."

"He is much beloved, a child marked by God." The padre crossed himself, then frowned briefly through the open door at the sky as if for a fraction of a second he was questioning God's common sense. "He lives with his grandparents and aunts and uncles and cousins. A happy family. It would be a pity to disturb their tranquillity."

"Where are his parents?"

"Gone. They left here years ago. They couldn't take the boy along because the authorities wouldn't allow it. You yourself are not from them, from the authorities?"

"No."

"Then I don't think I should answer any more questions. It might appear to be gossiping ... When tragedy strikes, everyone likes to talk about it, that's human nature. But it all happened in the distant past. Pablo doesn't remember his mother. To him everything is ten minutes ago, or an hour, or at most, yesterday. Even if he were normal, no one would remind him of her. She fell from grace."

"Does she communicate with the family?"

"No. She wouldn't want to, anyway, but even if she did, we have no telephones or mail service. There was talk of mail service once when someone was going to build here. Nothing came of either the building or the service. No matter, we survive."

"What about the boy's father?"

The padre considered the question in silence, squinting out at the sky again, this time for guidance. "He was an American. You see, Tula went away for a while to America. She had an unexpected opportunity to make a fortune. A fortune around here is very little, and when Tula saw her chance to go and get a job in America, she reached out and grabbed it."

"Who gave her the chance?"

"One Christmas a couple came along in a truck loaded with

old clothes and bedding and things like soap and canned goods to distribute to the more remote villagers in Baja. Tula persuaded the couple to take her back with them. She was very pretty, not too smart, but she could talk the ears off a donkey. So the people agreed and off she went. We heard nothing from her for a year or more. Then she came back married to a rich American and riding in a veritable chariot. My saints and sinners, what a vision she was, dressed like a princess and waving from the window of the chariot. Some of the women began screaming. They thought Tula had died and gone to heaven and this was her spirit. Oh, it was a great day. Everybody got drunk."

"What happened to the chariot?"

The padre's excitement faded. The great day was finished, everybody was sober, the chariot in ruins and the princess a long time missing.

"It never moved again. Its wheels got stuck in the sand and the engine broke down and there was no fuel anyway."

"And now it's the 'real house' the girl Valeria referred to in her marriage plans?"

"Yes. But you mustn't go there, you will disturb the family's tranquillity."

"Does Pablo live with them?"

"You most certainly can't talk to him. He doesn't understand. He is like a parrot, only repeating noises he hears. And the family will not want to discuss Tula, because she fell from grace . . . But I can see you're not hearing me, Tomas."

"I'm hearing you, padre," Aragon said. "I just can't afford to listen."

54

Seven

Only a few letters of the name still faintly visible on one side identified the ravaged hulk as Gilly's Dreamboat. The wheels had disappeared into the ground and most of the windows were broken. The paint had been scratched by chollas and creosote bushes, rusted by fog and salt air, blasted off by wind-driven sand.

On the roof was an old sun-bleached, urine-stained mattress. A lone chicken sat in the middle of it, casually pecking out the stuffing. It was the only living thing in sight. Yet Aragon was positive that there were people inside watching his approach with quiet hostility as if they'd already found out the purpose of his visit. It seemed impossible, though he knew it wasn't. In places where more sophisticated forms of communication were lacking, the grapevine was quick and efficient, and the fact that he'd seen no one outside the mission while he was talking to the padre meant nothing.

"Hello? Hello, in there! Can you hear me?"

He didn't expect an answer and none came. But he kept trying.

"Listen to me. I came from the United States looking for Mr. Lockwood, Byron James Lockwood. Can anyone give me some information about him or about Tula?"

If they could, they didn't intend to. The silence seemed even more profound: Tula's fall from grace had evidently been far and final.

"The padre will tell you that I mean no harm. And I'm offering money in return for information. Doesn't anyone want money?"

No one did. Money was of little value to people without a place to spend it or a desire to change their lot.

He waited another five minutes. The chicken pecking at the mattress stuffing remained the only sign of life.

The padre was waiting for him. He had opened another bottle of beer and his color was high and his eyes slightly out of focus.

"You're back very soon, Tomas."

"Yes."

"Our people are normally very friendly to strangers. If you were the exception, I apologize."

"I was, and thanks."

"You remind them of bad things and they're afraid. I am perhaps a little afraid myself. You're searching for the American, Lockwood?"

"Yes."

"Why?"

"Because Lockwood's wife wants him found." Lockwood's wife wasn't too accurate a description of Gilly but it served its purpose.

The padre looked shocked. "I thought Tula was—I didn't know he had another wife."

"Two other wives. Only one of them wants him found."

"Then Pablo is illegitimate?"

"Yes."

"All the more he is a child of God," the padre said, but he sounded shaken. "Of course, we will not tell any of the villagers about this. It would serve no purpose and the little boy might suffer unnecessarily. It is not easy being a child of God."

"How long did Lockwood stay here in the village?"

"Some four years or so. He was a nice man, kind to all the little ones and very fond of his son. He pretended the boy was normal, perhaps even to himself he pretended, I'm not sure."

"No, he knew the facts. The second Mrs. Lockwood had a letter from him referring to the boy."

"Then all the more he was a nice man, don't you think?"

"I think he must have been. Everyone I've talked to seems to have liked him." With the exception of Smedler, who didn't count because he never liked anybody. "Was he happy here, living under what for him were certainly primitive conditions?"

"But he was going to *change* the conditions. He had great plans for the village, great dreams. The mission would be restored, haciendas built, and a town square and a new pier to attract tourists in big boats. Also streets would be put in, real streets with beautiful names carved on stone pillars. The streets were laid out and some of the pillars already carved when the authorities arrived. Then suddenly it was all over."

"What happened?"

"He was arrested along with his partner, Jenkins, who was the real villain. But the authorities didn't bother to apportion blame on a percentage basis, eighty percent Jenkins, twenty percent Lockwood. No, they arrested them both equally."

"What was the charge?"

"It seems a lot of people were cheated. They sent money to buy lots on which haciendas were to be built, Jenlock Haciendas."

"A real estate swindle."

"I couldn't believe Mr. Lockwood deliberately swindled anyone. But what I believed was unimportant . . . The whole village came here to church to say farewell prayers for him. He was all dressed up for the occasion in his best suit and tie with a diamond tiepin in it, his fancy wristwatch and gold wedding ring and the ruby ring he wore on his little finger. He looked very splendid, like the day he arrived in the chariot. No one would have imagined he was being arrested, perhaps he could not really imagine it himself. Is this possible?"

"Yes."

"They took him away in a dirty old vehicle something like a bus with bars across the windows, a far cry from a chariot. When the bus left, he and Jenkins sat quietly, but Tula kept waving at us from the window precisely the way she'd waved on the day she and Lockwood arrived."

"Why did Tula go along?"

"I think to get away from the village, which bored her, and the child she was ashamed of, not so much to be with Lockwood."

"She couldn't be with him anyway, could she, if he was being sent to jail?"

"Oh yes, if she really wanted to. The jail in Rio Seco is very different from American jails I have seen in the cinema in Ensenada. Sometimes whole families live together, inside the walls. Or a prisoner, if he can afford it, may have his meals brought to him from outside or be visited by night ladies. The latter I don't approve. But the other thing—what harm is done? It is a more humane way to conduct a prison than the American way, don't you agree?"

"I agree that it's more humane for the prisoner, not necessarily for his family."

"Bear in mind that many of the men in prison have committed no crime, they are simply waiting for their cases to be heard. For most offenses no bail is allowed because under Mexican law there is no presumption of innocence such as in your country. Quite the contrary. A man is presumed guilty and is not entitled to a jury trial. His guilt or innocence, and his sentence, is decided by a magistrate. He can be kept in jail for a whole year before his case is even heard. This is very sad for the poor, who can't afford to pay bribes, but everyone expected when Mr. Lockwood was taken away that he would be back any week. We thought he still had some money, or that he could at least borrow some from his American friends in order to pay the magistrate for a favorable verdict. Perhaps he did. Perhaps he was released from prison and simply chose not to return here. We never heard from him again."

"Or from the girl?"

"No. A funny thing happened, though. Last fall, about a year ago, a sports fishing boat came down from the north coast and anchored in the bay. A man rowed ashore in a dinghy and left some boxes for the children containing clothes and toys and chewing gum and vitamin pills."

"Could they have been sent by Lockwood?"

"Possibly, though I would think he'd have included some more useful things. The children broke the toys in a week and fed the vitamin pills to the goats."

"Didn't you ask the man in the dinghy who sent him?"

"He couldn't speak Spanish and my English is very bad. We

have been the recipients of charity before—remember the truck which carried Tula to America?—so perhaps it was merely a coincidence that the boxes came to us."

"Coincidences happen, of course," Aragon said. "But in my profession they're usually viewed with suspicion."

"In my profession, also." The padre's smile was merely a further deepening of the grooves around his mouth. "So we view with suspicion, you and I. I wish it were not so."

"What happened to Jenkins?"

"No one knows or is in any hurry to find out. He had a bad effect on Mr. Lockwood. He would drive down to the village in a jeep, bringing rum and tequila and a briefcase full of drawings and blueprints and newspapers. Then after a few days he'd disappear again with more of Mr. Lockwood's money. Anyone but Mr. Lockwood would have perceived Jenkins' true character. He cared nothing about the villagers. He couldn't conceal how much he despised the people who couldn't read or write and didn't care. And to me, who could read and write on a higher level than his own, he made unkind remarks about being kicked out of the Church. I was never kicked out. I left. I left voluntarily because I committed a carnal sin."

The padre covered his face with his sleeve and Aragon wasn't sure whether he was wiping away tears or sweat, or whether he was attempting to hide his shame.

"Now I have told you everything, Tomas, more than you asked. I'm a silly old man full of beer and gossip."

"You've been a great help."

"I hope so. I'd like very much to see Mr. Lockwood again. We had many pleasant conversations and we used to listen to his radio until the batteries wore out. Will you give him a message for me? Tell him he is missed. Tell him— No, that will be enough. He is missed. I wouldn't really want him to know how much, it might make him feel bad if circumstances won't permit him to come back."

"You mean if he's still in jail?"

"Oh, I'm sure he won't be, a man of his worth, both moral and financial."

"I'm in no position to judge his moral worth," Aragon said. "However, I know that five years ago he needed money very badly. 'Desperately' was the word he used."

"But he had friends, did he not—rich American friends?"

"Rich American friends are hard to come by, especially when you're in trouble."

"You said he had a wife. She is also American?"

"Yes."

"And rich?"

"Yes."

"Perhaps he—"

"No. He didn't. She refused to send him any."

"That *is* a shame." The padre sighed, and wiped at his face again. "So you will go first to the Rio Seco jail to look for him. And if he's not there?"

"They must keep records."

"Oh, Tomas, you're a dreamer. Records of what? Of who paid how much to which magistrate?"

"The girl is the only lead I have."

"So off you go. When?"

"I should get back to Rio Seco late tonight. Right now I'd like to look around the village."

"I would accompany you, Tomas, but I'm a little unsteady on my feet and this is siesta time. The sun is very hot. Do you have a hat to wear?"

"No."

"Here, you can have mine."

"No," Aragon said. "No thank you." It would be unfair to the gentle little man to be reminded of him by a case of head lice.

"Have a safe journey, Tomas. Our visit has been so enjoyable I hate to see it end. Will you ever come back?"

"Not likely."

"I've reached the age where anyone who lets me talk seems like an old friend. By listening to my memories, you have become part of them. I hope you don't mind."

"I like the idea very much."

"Goodbye, friend."

"Good health and God's blessing, padre."

The two men shook hands. Then Aragon started walking down toward the pier and the row of shacks beside the abandoned fish cannery.

The severity of the sun had closed the village down as completely as if a bad storm had struck or an epidemic of plague. There was no sign of activity anywhere, even on the sloop riding at anchor in the bay. Only the sound of a crying child from inside one of the shacks indicated that they were occupied.

Beyond the shacks, on a knoll overlooking the bay, he found what he was looking for, the beginning—and the ending—of Jenlock Haciendas. "Streets would be put in," the padre had said, "real streets with beautiful names carved on stone pillars." The streets, if they had ever existed, were buried under sand, but the identifying pillars remained unchanged. The same wind that blasted the paint off Dreamboat had merely kept the pillars wiped as clean as tombstones in a carefully tended cemetery. Each way was a dead end, avenues east and west, streets north and south: Calle Jardin Encanto, Calle Paloma de Paz, Avenida Cielito Verde, Avenida Corona de Oro, Avenida Gilda.

"Avenida Gilda." He repeated the name aloud as if the sound of it might make it more believable. The stone was perfectly symmetrical and the carving done with great care and skill in Gothic letters.

He went back to his car. Through the open door of the mission he could hear the padre snoring. He took the remaining bottles of beer inside and left them on the table. The Blessed Virgin gave him one fierce final stare.

He reached Rio Seco about one o'clock in the morning and checked into a hotel. It was too late to phone Gilly. Besides, he had very little to tell her and nothing she'd like to hear: B. J. and his partner, Jenkins, had been taken to jail; the boy, Pablo, was not only crippled but retarded; and in the middle of a couple of billion cubic feet of sand was a tombstone with her name carved on it.

He went to bed.

Eight

The jail was in the center of Rio Seco as if it had been the first structure and the rest of the city had been built around it. It was shaped like a roundhouse and circled by stone walls twenty-five or thirty feet high which gave it its name: the stone quarry. LA CANTERA, Penitenciaria del Estado was carved above the main entrance where Aragon stood with the other people waiting to be admitted.

In spite of the earliness of the hour, traffic was heavy and the crowd outside the jail was large—a few men of varying ages, but mostly women carrying babies and straw bags and packages wrapped in newspaper, and a handful of prostitutes in miniskirts and maxiwigs. Children played in the street, oblivious to the honking of horns and squealing of tires, or ran up the stone steps and slid down the iron banisters. Apart from the crowd an older American couple, neatly dressed and quiet, stood with their arms locked as if they were holding each other up.

One of the three guards on duty, a young man wearing a cowboy hat and oversized boots that looked like hand-me-downs from a bigger brother, fielded questions: "Ten more minutes, I don't make the rules, señora . . . Carlos Gonzalez got out last week . . . Café opens at nine . . . You can go home, girls, it's too early. Give the boys a chance to wash up . . . If Gonzalez left a message,

I don't know about it . . . Anyone want a shouter? Ten cents for a shouter, fifteen cents for a first-class shouter."

The American man held up his hand. "Yes. Please."

"How much?"

"Fifteen cents."

"Name?"

"Sandra Boyd."

"Sandra Boyd. Okay, anyone else? . . . Ten cents for Cecilio Martinez . . . Five cents for Manuel Ysidro. That's a whisper, maybe you don't want him to hear . . . Ten for Fernando Escobar . . . Ten, Inocente Santana. We got a lot of Inocentes in this place. Not a guilty in sight, ha ha . . . Carlos Gonzalez. You're wasting your money, señora. I told you, he's gone. Okay, ten for Gonzalez."

"Lockwood," Aragon said. "B. J. Lockwood and Harry Jenkins."

"That's two names."

"Yes."

"You can't have one shouter for two names. You must have one shouter for each name."

"All right, thirty cents."

At eight-thirty the gates of the Quarry opened and the crowd surged inside. No attempt was made to question or search anyone or to examine packages. It would have been impossible under the circumstances. The pushing and shoving and screaming reminded Aragon of doorbuster sales at some of the stores back home.

Within the walls, similar high-pressure merchandising was taking place. The prison peddlers began hawking their wares: pottery, leatherwork, novelties, food and drink, children's toys. A trio of *mariachis* singing "Guadalajara, Guadalajara," gave a fiesta atmosphere to the scene.

The *mariachis* picked Aragon as their first mark of the morning.

"You want to hear a special song, señor?"

"No thanks."

"We sing anything you say."

"Not right now."

"We know a hundred songs."

Aragon paid twenty-five cents not to hear any of them.

The cellblocks were built in a circle around a huge recreation yard, where a soccer game was in progress. While he waited in line at the iron-grilled information window he watched the soccer game. Both sides were dressed alike, so it was difficult to follow. But it was a very lively spectacle, since there were no referees.

Guadalajara, Guadalajara.

You buy a taco, señor? An empanada?

Real, hand-tooled leather purses and belts at prices so low it is a crime.

Balloons, dolls, madonnas, bracelets, cigarettes.

A fight broke out between two men peddling identical calfskin wallets. Compared to the soccer game, it was dull and half-hearted and attracted little attention. Obviously the inmates had more interest in soccer than in fistfights that consisted mainly of loud words and soft blows.

The shouters were already at work:

"Oswaldo Fernandez, hey, Oswaldo Fernandez, hey, Fernandez."

"Cruz Rivera, ay ay Cruz, ay ay Rivera, ay ay ay ay Cruz Rivera."

"B. J. Lockwood ... Lock—wood."

"Harry Jenkins ... You are wanted, Harry Jenkins."

"Juanita Maria Placencia, come here, Jua—ni—ta!"

"Sandra Boyd, if you please ... Sandra Boyd ... Sandra Boyd."

"Amelio Gutierrez, answer to your name."

When Aragon's turn came he presented his credentials to the uniformed man at the information window. After consulting with his colleagues, the man sent a runner to summon the assistant to the assistant to the warden himself.

The new arrival introduced himself as Superintendent Perdiz. "These two Americans you are asking about, I never heard of them. It would be better for you to come back later when the warden is here."

"How much later?"

"Wednesday. He works very hard and needs long weekends to recuperate at his beach house."

"Who's in charge when the warden's away?"

"The assistant warden. He'll be back tomorrow, Tuesday. He

doesn't need such long weekends because his responsibilities are not so great."

"He's got a beach house too, I suppose."

"No. He likes to go to the mountains. The air is more invigorating. Here in Rio Seco we have bad air. Do you smell it? Phew!"

Aragon smelled it. Traffic odors, people odors, jail odors, exhaust fumes, sweat, garlic, urine, cigarette smoke, antiseptic.

"Phew," Perdiz said again. "Don't you think so?"

"Yes."

"Then you understand the need for long weekends out of town?"

"Of course."

"So now we are in complete agreement. A man, even one in a lowly position like mine, needs a country house for a breath of sea or mountain air on the weekends. I'd like to buy such a place but my salary won't allow it."

"Would ten dollars help?"

"A little more might inspire me to go and search the files personally. What do you think my personal attention is worth?"

"Fifteen dollars."

"That's most kind of you."

Perdiz accepted the bribe with solemn dignity. After all, it was part of the system, paying a *mordida* to *influyentes,* and he was an *influyente.* "You wait here."

Aragon waited. He watched the soccer game some more and bought a wallet from the loser of the fistfight, a can of ginger ale and a doll made of two withered oranges with cloves marking its features and dried red chiles for arms and legs. He didn't know why he'd bought such a ridiculous thing until he held it in his hand and studied it for a while: it looked like Pablo, round-eyed and vacant-faced, untouched, untouchable.

The shouters were still at work. At least one of them had brought results—the American couple were talking to a pale stringy-haired young woman wearing a ragged poncho that reached almost to her ankles. The man was doing most of the talking, the older woman was crying, the younger one looked bored.

Perdiz returned. Nowhere in the files was there any mention of B. J. Lockwood.

"You should have some record of him," Aragon said. "He was arrested."

"How do you know he was arrested?"

"I was told."

"Who told you?"

"A priest."

"A priest. Then it's very likely true that he was arrested. But maybe it was a mistake. Maybe he didn't do anything wrong, so they let him go. If we kept records on everyone who never did anything wrong, we'd have a jail full of paper. A paper jail, isn't that a funny idea?"

"A real rib-tickler," Aragon said. Gilly was now an unofficial contributor to a beach house or maybe a mountain cabin, but she wasn't any closer to B. J. "What about Harry Jenkins?"

"I could find nothing concerning him either. Truthfully—you want truthfully?"

"Yes."

"All right, truthfully. We don't like to keep records on Americans. It's bad for international relations. Consider which is more important, a few pieces of paper or a great war between nations."

"I don't think anyone would start even a very small war over Harry Jenkins."

"One never knows. Peace today, war tomorrow."

"Yes. Well, thank you for your trouble, Perdiz." *And may your beach house be swept away by a tidal wave and your mountain cabin buried under an avalanche.*

He began pushing his way through the crowd in the direction of the main gate. When he passed the American couple he saw that both the man and the older woman were now crying, but the girl hadn't changed expression. She was absently tying, untying and retying a couple of strands of her hair. On impulse Aragon handed her the dried orange-and-chili doll that looked like Pablo. She immediately picked out the cloves that were his eyes and popped them in her mouth. Nobody said anything.

He had almost reached the main gate when he felt a hand touch his back between his shoulder blades. He turned abruptly, expecting to catch an inept pickpocket. Instead, he saw a Mexican woman about thirty, with dark despondent eyes and wiry black hair that seemed to have sprung out of her scalp in revolt. Her arms and hands were covered with scars of various sizes and shapes and colors, as if the wounds had occurred at different times under different circumstances.

Her voice had the hoarseness of someone who talked too loud and too long. "I heard a shouter calling for Harry Jenkins. I said, 'Who hired you?' and he said, 'An American with big glasses and a blue striped shirt.' That's you."

"That's me. Tomas Aragon."

"Why do you want to see Harry?"

"Why do you want to know why I want to see Harry?"

"I'm Emilia, Harry's good friend. Very good, special. Someday we will be married in the church but that must wait. Right now I am in and he is out. Before that, I was out and he was in, and before that, we were both in. What did Harry do to you?"

"Nothing."

"Then why are you looking for him?"

"Actually I'm looking for a friend of his. I thought Harry might give me—or sell me—some information."

"You buy information?"

"Sometimes."

Her lips parted enough to reveal two slightly protruding front teeth. It was the closest Emilia ever came to a smile. "I have information."

"What kind?"

"All kinds. The best. I've been around the Quarry off and on since I was fifteen. When I go away they beg me, 'Emilia Ontiveros, come back, come back.' If I say no, they invent charges to force me to come back because I am such a fine cook. I am the head cook in the Quarry café."

That explained the scars. They were burns and cuts accumulated throughout the years.

"Do you have information about Harry Jenkins, Emilia?"

"He is a snake. That much I give you free. The rest will be more expensive."

"I'd like to talk to you. Isn't there some place we could have a little more privacy?"

"There's a talking room. It will cost you money, fifty cents. But a dollar would be better."

It was probably the primary law of the Quarry: a dollar was better than fifty cents but not as good as two dollars, which was vastly inferior to ten.

For a dollar they were given a couple of wooden stools in the corner of a room half filled with people, most of them in the fifty-cent, or standing, class. Emilia sat with her scarred hands clenched in her lap.

"A snake," she repeated. "Though you would never guess it to look at him. Such honest blue eyes, such even teeth."

"Do you know where he's living?"

"Ha! I have people keeping track of him every day, every minute. I know what clothes he wears, what he eats for breakfast. He can't buy a pack of cigarettes without me finding out. What a fool he was to think he could leave me cold after I paid good money for his release. When I leave this place again, I'm going to mash him like a turnip."

"I thought you intended to get married in the church."

"First I mash him like a turnip. *Then* we get married."

She was unmistakably serious. No matter where he was, Harry's future didn't look too bright.

"Marriage might improve my temper," she added thoughtfully. "I lose it at the stove, at the pots and pans, because they burn me. Then I throw them and they burn me again, and on it goes, back and forth. Do you think marriage has an improving effect?"

"Occasionally."

"How much are you planning to pay me?"

"You haven't told me anything useful yet."

"What do you want to know?"

"You said you and Jenkins served time together."

"That's how we met. These two Americans were brought in one day and as soon as I saw Harry my insides started spinning."

"The other American was Lockwood?"

Emilia nodded. "Him, what a crybaby, always fussing about this and that. The guards had to give him stuff to shut him down. Harry was a real man, pretending he didn't care what the authorities did to him or how long they kept him there."

"What was the charge against him?"

"Something silly like cheating. It's the custom. Somebody cheats you, you cheat somebody else."

"How did Jenkins get out?"

"Me. I had some money saved—the head cook's pay is pretty good and there's nothing pretty to spend it on in this place. When I finished serving my sentence I rented a nice apartment and then I went and paid Harry's fine and we set up housekeeping. For a while we had a rosy time. But my rosy times never last. As soon as the money ran out, so did Harry. Or tried to. I caught him packing and beat him up, not bad, just enough to put him in the hospital. He didn't squeal on me—he knew he had it coming—but the doctor at the hospital reported me to the police and they brought me back here to the Quarry. Everybody was glad to see me, of course, because my tamale pie is the best in town . . . How much are you going to pay me?"

"For telling me your tamale pie is the best in town? Nothing. It's not the kind of information that's worth anything to me."

"What kind do you want? You name it, it's yours. See, I'm saving up so I can buy my way out of this place and go back with Harry."

"And mash him like a turnip."

"Maybe not. Maybe my heart will melt when I see him again."

Aragon wouldn't have bet a nickel on it. Emilia's temper probably had a lower boiling point than her heart. "Is Jenkins still living in the apartment you rented?"

"How could he afford an apartment without my help? No, he has a little room over the shoemaker's shop, Reynoso's, on Avenida Gobernador. It's a low neighborhood, lots of thieves and prostitutes, but Harry hasn't anything to steal and the prostitutes don't bother him, because he's broke. How am I sure? My spies are here, there and everywhere, watching. Right this minute he is"— Emilia consulted a man's wristwatch which she fished out of the front of her dress—"sleeping. That's Harry for you. Everybody else running around working and Harry in bed snoring his head off."

"What does he do when he's not sleeping?"

"Hangs out at bars and cafés, especially the places where Americans go, El Domino, Las Balatas, El Alegre. He's not a drunk, liquor's not one of his weaknesses, he goes there on business."

"What kind of business?"

"Whatever he thinks of. He's very smart but he has bad luck.

And tourists aren't as easy as they used to be in the old days when all he had to do was make up a few little stories. Expenses keep going up and up, and tourists keep getting more and more suspicious and stingy."

Aragon thought of the Hilton price he'd paid for the shack at Viñadaco and he wasn't surprised that the tourists were getting more wary of Harry's little stories.

He said, "What happened to Lockwood?"

"I don't know. Suddenly he left. That was long before I paid Harry's fine and got him out."

"Did he come back to visit Jenkins?"

"Why should he? They weren't friends, they were partners. He blamed Harry for leading him into trouble. How can you lead someone who doesn't want to go?"

"Did you notice whether Lockwood had any visitors?"

"There are always Americans shut up in this place, and the American consulate sends somebody over to check on them from time to time. Maybe it was one of the consulate that got Lockwood released."

"Did his case ever come to trial?"

"It was a single case, him and Harry together, when they were brought in. But when the magistrate finally heard it, there was just Harry. Lockwood had disappeared."

"Do you think he died?"

"A lot of people do," Emilia said philosophically. "He was an old man, anyway, more than fifty, always throwing up from his stomach."

"Didn't Jenkins try to find out what happened to him?"

"If he did he never told me. We had more interesting things to talk about in our rosy times. In the not-so-rosy we didn't speak to each other at all."

She repeated Jenkins' address, Avenida Gobernador above the shop of Reynoso the shoemaker. Aragon thanked her and gave her ten dollars. She didn't seem too pleased at the amount, but at least she didn't try to mash him like a turnip.

Nine

He returned to the Hotel Castillo, stopping at the desk for his key and a map of the city, the kind which gas stations back home used to give away free. The map cost two dollars, the key was free. From his room he tried, for the second time that day, to put through a call to Gilly. All the lines were in use, on business, the *telefonista* implied, much more urgent than his.

Over lunch and beer at the hotel café he studied the map of Rio Seco. Avenida Gobernador was within walking distance and he would have liked to walk, both for exercise and to avoid the insanities of the city traffic. (One of the oddities of the automotive age was how such good-natured, slow-moving people could become irascible speed freaks behind the wheel of a car.) But the Avenida paralleled the course of the river for several miles and he had no way of knowing on what part of it Reynoso's shop was located. It was not in the telephone directory or on the hotel's list of shops and services.

He found out why when he reached it. It was hardly more than a hole in the wall on the edge of the red-light district where porno bars alternated with the rows of prostitutes' cubicles. The neighborhood was quiet, and Reynoso's place closed. Sex as well as shoemakers took a siesta.

A boy about Pablo's age offered to watch his car to make sure nobody stole the hub caps and windshield wipers and radio antenna. "Hey, man, watch your car? One quarter for watching your car, man."

"Who's going to watch you?" Aragon said.

He meant it as a joke but the boy took it seriously. "My brother José. He's working the other side of the street."

"Why aren't you in school?"

"It's a holiday."

"What holiday?"

"I don't know. Somebody just told me, 'Hey, man, you don't got to go to school today, it's a holiday.' Watch your car for a quarter?"

"All right."

He paid the money. The boy climbed on the hood of the car, leaned back against the windshield and lit the butt of a cigar he'd picked up from the road.

Aragon said, "You watch cars around here all the time?"

"Sure, man."

"I bet you know a lot of people in the neighborhood."

"I got eyes, don't I?"

"I'm looking for an American named Harry Jenkins. I was told he lives in a room above Reynoso's."

"Whoever told you's got eyes too. That's where he lives, Harry Jenkins. Some cheapskate. Never gave me a dime."

"Reynoso's shop is closed."

"Yeah, I know."

"For one of the dimes Jenkins never gave you, will you tell me how I can get up to his room?"

"You a hustler, man?"

"Let's just say that the members of my profession are sometimes called hustlers."

"Yeah? Okay, then. There's an alley four, five doors down, takes you straight to Reynoso's outside stairs."

The boy pocketed the dime and settled back against the windshield to enjoy the final inch of the cigar.

Jenkins' door was locked. When Aragon knocked on it, it felt flimsy as though it would collapse like cardboard if he leaned against it too heavily. He wrote a note and pushed it underneath the door:

72

Mr. Jenkins:

I am offering a fair price for any information you might have about B. J. Lockwood. If you are interested, please contact me at the Hotel Castillo.

T. C. Aragon

He returned to the hotel and tried for the third time to put through a call to Gilly. The *telefonista* must have had a refreshing siesta, she sounded almost human: "You wish to speak personally to Mrs. Marco Decker, is that correct?"

"Yes."

"I may have a line for you now. Hold on."

After about five minutes of back-and-forth chatter in two languages, a man answered the phone. "Hello." A certain note of petulance in the man's tone identified him as Reed Robertson, Marco Decker's nurse.

"I have a person-to-person call for Mrs. Marco Decker. Is Mrs. Decker there?"

"Hold on." Reed raised the pitch of his voice about an octave. "This is Mrs. Decker, operator. I'll take the call."

"Your party is on the line, sir. Go ahead."

"Hello, Reed."

"That you, Aragon?"

"Yes."

"She's in the pool. Violet Smith just took her out a robe, so she'll be here in a minute. Listen, amigo, she's burned up because she hasn't heard from you."

"She burns easy. It's only Monday."

"Any trace of B. J.?"

" 'Trace' just about covers it. I found his ex-partner, though."

"Harry Jenkins."

"I gather Mrs. Decker has confided in you."

"The old girl has to talk to somebody. It was a toss-up between me and Violet Smith. I won. If you want to call it winning."

"What do you call it?"

"I call it a living," Reed said. "Speaking of living, where's Jenkins doing his, in some castle in the sky?"

73

"Over Reynoso's shoemaking shop on Avenida Gobernador. I might say he's on his uppers if I went in for bad puns."

"So Jenlock Haciendas never got off the ground."

"No. All the other news is bad, too."

"How bad?"

Gilly came on the line. "Aragon? What's this about bad? Have you found B. J.?"

"No."

"That's not exactly bad, is it? I mean, it's just nothing. How is that bad?"

"B. J. seems to have disappeared."

"From where?"

"The jail in Rio Seco."

"Did you say *jail*?"

"Yes."

"What was he doing in jail?"

"Like all the others in there, he was waiting to get out."

"Don't get sharp with me, dammit."

"I'm trying not to," Aragon said. "I don't like delivering news like this any more than you like receiving it."

"Why was he sent to jail? B. J. wouldn't hurt a fly."

"Flies don't invest money in real estate developments. People do, and when they discover they've been swindled they complain to the police. B. J. and Jenkins were picked up in Bahía de Ballenas. While they were waiting trial B. J. disappeared. One of the other inmates told me he'd been ill and upset and the guards had to give him stuff to calm him down. 'Stuff' was the word used. It could have been anything."

"Oh God, poor B. J."

She began to cry. Aragon could hear Reed trying to soothe her: *Buck up, old girl. Stop it now. Here, here's a drink. That's a good girl . . .*

When things quieted down, Aragon continued, "I may get more information tonight or tomorrow. I haven't talked to Harry Jenkins, but I found out where he's living and left a note for him."

"Left a *note*? You should have waited for him, camped on his doorstep if necessary."

"He didn't have a doorstep. He didn't even have much of a door."

"Give me his phone number. I want to talk to him myself."

"I guess I'm not getting through to you, Mrs. Decker. Jenkins is broke. That's the main reason I expect to hear from him. I offered him money for information about B. J."

There was a long interval of silence. Then, "Where's the girl, Tula?"

"I have no recent news about her. When the two men were arrested she went with them to Rio Seco. The word is that she wanted to get away from Bahía de Ballenas and the child, too."

"Away from her own child?"

"He's retarded as well as crippled, Mrs. Decker . . . Now don't start crying again. The boy's safe, he's being looked after by relatives. Mexican families are very close-knit, as I mentioned to you before, and retarded children aren't considered undesirable."

"Have you nothing decent, nothing pleasant to tell me?"

"I think it's both decent and pleasant that Pablo is being taken care of. He's luckier in many ways than his American cousins."

"How long ago did they leave him there?"

"Four years. He's eight now, chronologically. Mentally, perhaps three. There is no way he could fit into your life, Mrs. Decker."

"I never thought he could," she said quietly. "I just hoped a little bit. If it were only a matter of his being crippled, I could have paid for doctors, operations . . . Now, of course, I realize that it's impossible. I wish I'd never been told of his existence. Maybe B. J. told me deliberately to rouse my sympathy so I'd send him the money he asked for. If I could believe that, it would make it easier for me to accept—what I'm afraid you're going to find out."

"Which is?"

"That he's dead, he died in jail and they dragged him out and buried him like a common criminal." He heard her take a long deep breath as if to regain control of herself. "Okay, all the news is bad so far. What's the next step?"

"I'll talk to Jenkins."

"Suppose he doesn't know anything?"

"Then I'd better quit wasting your money and come home."

"Call me after you've seen him. And thanks, by the way, for leveling with me, even though I didn't like it. The truth hurts . . . I wonder who first discovered that."

"Probably Adam."

"The little boy, does he seem happy?"

"He seems not unhappy. He gets affection and enough food to eat, and he has children to play with who aren't much more advantaged than he is. You could present a bigger problem to him than any he has now, Mrs. Decker."

"Yes, I see. It was really stupid of me after all this time to get the idea that—well, anyway, thanks again. And call me."

"I will."

She hung up. Reed was leaning against the wall with his arms crossed on his chest, watching her. She had never realized before what cruel little eyes he had. They didn't match the rest of his face, which smiled a lot.

"You were practically screaming at one point," Reed said. "Women should learn to modulate their voices."

"Why?"

"So people will assume they're ladies. Also to make it harder for eavesdroppers like Violet Smith to hear everything. Violet Smith is ninety-eight percent ears and mouth and two percent common sense. She could be dangerous."

"I didn't say anything she can't broadcast to the world if she wants to."

"Fear not, she'll want to. Wait until the next show-and-tell meeting at her church—you and B. J. will be the star attractions, with the kid thrown in for a touch of pathos. By the way, you're not fooling me for a minute. And if Aragon weren't such a boy scout, you wouldn't be fooling him, either."

"How am I trying to fool anyone?"

"The kid. You wouldn't touch him with a ten-foot pole even if he had a perfect physique and an IQ of a hundred and fifty."

"You're malicious, you're really malicious."

"That's why we get along so well. Malice is something we both understand. Now, Violet Smith isn't malicious. She's just dumb and self-righteous, which is a lot harder to cope with. You'd better go and have a talk with her right now. Lay it on the line but keep it light, casual. Don't let on that it matters too much."

"*You're* giving *me* orders?"

"Suggestions."

"They sounded like orders."

76

"No, my orders sound quite different," Reed said. "You may find that out."

The cleaning woman and day maid had left and Violet Smith was alone in the kitchen, cooking dinner and watching TV.

"Turn that thing off," Gilly said.

"I'm in the middle of a murder."

"Turn it off."

"My stars, you needn't shout. I didn't know this was top priority."

"You do now."

Violet Smith turned off the set, grumbling. "My programs are always being interrupted, phones ringing, Mr. Decker buzzing—"

"Speaking of phones, did you listen in on the extension to my conversation with Mr. Aragon?"

"I told you, I'm in the middle of a murder, which is a heap more interesting than anything Mr. Aragon has to say."

"Answer the question. Did you listen in?"

"No. Honest injun, though I'm not supposed to say that. It's ethnic. I heard all about ethnic from a black man at church. People shouldn't use ethnic expressions like 'eeny meeny miney mo, catch a nigger by the toe,' or—"

"At these church meetings of yours, what do you talk about when it's your turn?"

"My life."

"Including the part of it that takes place here?"

"Here it's your life, not mine."

"Then you wouldn't mention my personal affairs in front of the group?"

"No."

"That's good. Because what goes on in this house is my own business and I don't care to have any of it repeated in the name of the Lord or soul cleansing or mental health or any damn thing at all. Understand?"

Violet Smith stood mute as marble.

"Do you understand?"

"I'd like to get back to my murder now, if you don't mind."

"Do that."

"Thank you," said Violet Smith.

She waited until she heard Gilly go down the hall and open the door of her husband's room. Then she picked up the phone and dialed the number she had just checked in the directory. The voice that answered was one Violet Smith greatly admired, so soft and sweet and the opposite of Gilly's.

"Hello?"

"Is that Mrs. Lockwood?"

"Yes. Who's this?"

"Violet Smith, your friend from church."

"Oh, of course."

"You said you'd like me to come over sometime for a little chat."

"Yes."

"Well, I think this is the time, Mrs. Lockwood."

It took Marco an hour to eat a meal that would hardly have nourished a sparrow.

Sometimes Gilly sat with him in silence, feeding him his sparrow-sized bites and watching him chew so slowly and awkwardly that she felt her own teeth grinding in frustration. Sometimes she turned on the TV, which Marco didn't like because he had trouble seeing with only one functioning eye; and sometimes she just talked, dipping into the present or cutting up the past into small digestible pieces.

Consciously or not, she left out a few things about her past and added a few. In the main, though, it was pretty straight talk. During the months of her husband's illness she'd covered a great many of her fifty years, but more and more her conversation was about those she'd spent with B. J. For the past week it had been almost exclusively about B. J. She talked of falling in love with him right away, bingo, at first sight. She never believed such a thing could happen, to her of all people. He wasn't much to look at, he had no line of fast talk, he couldn't play games or dance very well or any of the things that might draw a woman's attention. And he was married. Happily married, or so his wife claimed when she came to Gilly and told her to leave him alone. Leave him alone. How could she? As long as B. J. was alive in this world she could never have left him alone.

The sick man listened. He had no way of stopping her except by going to sleep or pretending to, and he seldom did either. Gilly had such an impassioned way of talking that she could make a visit from the plumber sound like an earthshaking event. Gilly's plumber wouldn't be handsome or witty or charming, but he would have an indefinable irresistible something. She couldn't bear to let him go—but at twenty bucks an hour she had to.

"I'm giving Reed a few days off," she said. "He's getting restless and bossy, he needs a change. I've put in a call for a substitute nurse. I'll ask for two if you think you need them."

The forefinger of his right hand moved. *One would be enough.*

"Just one then. We can manage. I usually give you your shots, anyway. Do you need another right now or can you wait?"

Now.

She was very expert at it, better than Reed, who was inclined to hurry, as though he had a ward full of patients waiting for him.

"There. That will help you chew. Let's try the fish. It might be better tonight. I asked Violet Smith to pour a lot of booze on it ... When Reed gets like this, you know, sort of pushy and insolent, a little holiday snaps him back ... B. J. and I were going on a holiday when— But I've bored you with that story a dozen times, haven't I?"

Yes.

"I went out and bought this marvelous motor home as a surprise for his birthday so the two of us could drive up to British Columbia, where my folks came from. I called it Dreamboat and I had the name printed on it as a custom touch. Well, you know what happened, don't you? B. J. added a custom touch of his own. Tula her name was, not as pretty as Dreamboat. Neither was she. All I can really remember about her is a lot of black bushy hair and greasy skin. Oh yes, and her fingernails. She kept them painted bright-red but her hands were always grimy. How she got to B. J. I don't know. The why was easy enough. She was hungry. She wanted to live like in the movies and there was only one way to do it. So she did it. In the end she lost him too, not to another woman but to a con man named Harry Jenkins, can you beat it?"

No, he couldn't beat it, or tie it, or come close. He could only listen.

"It's funny when you think about it—Henry Jenkins took

B. J. from Tula the way she took him from me and I took him from Ethel. We just sort of passed him along from one to another like a used car. Even Ethel, Ethel the Good, she probably took him from somebody else. There was always someone waiting, wanting to use B. J. Where did it all start? The day he was born, the day the car came off the assembly line ... Come on, try the mashed potatoes. Violet Smith makes them with real cream."

He wouldn't. She didn't.

"I think B. J.'s real weakness was the way he had of living completely in the present, never looking back to learn from experience, never looking ahead to see consequences. Somebody like Harry Jenkins could have picked him out of a crowd in half a minute. By the way, Aragon has found out where Jenkins is living in Rio Seco. He'll be talking to him tonight or tomorrow. The trail's getting really hot now. Isn't that exciting? Aren't you excited?"

I am afraid.

He stopped chewing. He refused to swallow. He closed his eye.

Ten

About the time Aragon would be thinking of going to bed back home, Rio Seco was just opening up for the night. From the window of his hotel room he watched the street below. There were crowds of people, including whole families, in the cafés and markets and in a long line in front of the cinema. The curio and art dealers, the silversmiths and street vendors and sandal makers were starting the real business of the day.

Except for an hour off for dinner, Aragon had spent the evening waiting to hear from Harry Jenkins. He'd written a long letter to his wife and a short note to Smedler. He read the evening paper, *La Diaria,* and twice he went down to the desk to ask for messages. There were none. A third time he went down for a can of insecticide to get rid of the mosquitoes. What might have been an unusual request in most hotels was taken for granted at the Castillo. The insecticide was provided by the night clerk free of charge. "We have this problem with the bugs, sir. When we kill them, they come back. When we don't kill them, they don't go away."

"I understand."

The clerk looked surprised. "You do?"

"I'm a lawyer."

"That's it, then. Lawyers understand everything, even bugs, yes?"

"Especially bugs," Aragon said. "Good night."

He sprayed the room until the mosquitoes were all dead. Then he had to open the window to get rid of the fumes, and a whole new swarm of mosquitoes entered. He settled down with some beer to match them, pint for pint. For every pint they took from him, he drank a pint to replace the fluid.

The din from the street below increased in volume. He almost missed hearing the knock on his door shortly after midnight.

He unlocked the door. "Mr. Jenkins?"

"That's me, Harry Jenkins."

"I'm Tom Aragon. Come in, won't you?"

"Don't mind if I do, seeing as you offered some reimbursement for my time and trouble. That's correct, isn't it?"

"Yes."

Jenkins closed the door behind him. He was a small thin man in his mid-forties, dressed in a dark-blue suit frayed at the cuffs and so shiny across the seat of his pants that he looked as though he'd slipped in a pool of melted wax. "So you want to talk about B. J., right?"

"No. I want you to talk about him."

"Same difference, like they say. After I read your note I sat me down to do some thinking. Here's how it came out. One of B. J.'s old big-shot friends got a pang of conscience for not helping him out before and now he, or she, wants to buy a little peace of mind."

"Go on."

"Any damn fool knows that that's the only piece of something not for sale in the world. So I figure it has to be a she, since they don't go by the rules of reason. The question is, What she?"

"I thought the question was, How much do you know and what is it worth?"

"You have yourself a point there, laddie."

Jenkins moved quickly and gracefully across the room, balancing on the balls of his feet like a featherweight boxer between punches. Everything about him seemed to be in motion except his eyes. They had no more life in them than patches of gray suede.

"If you read my note this afternoon," Aragon said, "what took you so long to get here?"

"A place like this cramps my style. I don't even have the

clothes for it. I had to borrow the suit from a friend. It's not much of a suit, but then, he's not much of a friend, either."

"Clothes don't matter much any more."

"They do in my business."

"What's your business, Mr. Jenkins?"

"It varies. Right now things are slow, but I'm tossing a few ideas back and forth." He smoothed his thinning hair across the bald spot on top of his head as if to protect the source of the ideas. "I can't work at an ordinary job. Don't have the stomach for it. Or the papers. The immigration boys are a nervous bunch. One little mistake and they jump you."

"Jenlock Haciendas was more than a little mistake, wouldn't you say?"

"I'd be the first to say it. I got in over my head. My other business ventures are less ambitious."

"Sit down, will you?"

"Thanks."

"Join me in a beer?"

"Might as well, I guess." Jenkins stood at the window looking down at the street. "I'd like to get out of this crappy town."

"Why don't you?"

"There was a little episode in Albuquerque and maybe a couple of other places. Not everybody shares my philosophy of forgive and forget . . . How'd you track me down, anyway?"

"Went to the Quarry and hired a shouter. One of the inmates came over to talk to me."

"Emilia."

"Yes."

"What'd she tell you?"

"That when she's released she's going to mash you like a turnip."

"She will, too," Jenkins said gloomily. "Unless I get out before she does. I always had a weakness for fiery women, but now I think I'm over it." He took a sip of beer, grimacing, as though the stuff had the bitter taste of regrets. "I have to shake this town. The cops, the immigration boys, Emilia's relatives—I can't walk around the block without being hassled. My only chance is meeting up with a well-heeled sucker at one of the American bars. Funny how Americans who wouldn't give each other the time of day in

Chicago or Louisville become bosom pals over a couple of drinks at the Domino Club. Well, all I need is the right bosom." Jenkins turned and studied Aragon carefully for a moment. "It's too bad we know each other. It cramps my style. I prefer to deal with strangers."

"I bet you do."

"Friends are murder in this business . . . I wouldn't mind another beer if you were offering any, laddie."

"I'm offering." Aragon opened another can. "How did you get mixed up in something as big as the Jenlock Haciendas project?"

"Innocent-like. I mean, I didn't walk into it. I just stood there and it grew up around me."

"Is that what you told the magistrate?"

"I tried to. My Spanish isn't too good. Maybe he didn't understand me."

"Or maybe he did."

"It was true, so help me. I'd been hearing plenty of talk about how Baja was due for a big boom as soon as the new highway was finished. I borrowed some money, rented a jeep and went down to have a look-see. Well, the boom's on now and it's big, so I was right about that. The wrong part was the location and B. J. . . . To this day I don't know how I managed to get lost. But I did. And that's how I arrived at Bahía de Ballenas. Ever hear of it?"

"I've heard of it."

"Well, there was B. J., living in a super-deluxe motor home and looking like money. A bunch of money. It went to my head. No drink ever invented could go to my head like that. It wasn't like getting drunk alone and sleeping it off. B. J. stayed right with me. Every idea I came up with, he came up with an improvement. Then I improved on the improvement, until finally there it was, Jenlock Haciendas, bigger than both of us. I didn't have sense enough to be scared. I was not only out of my league, I didn't even know what game I was playing."

"It's called fraud."

"Wouldn't have mattered, anyway. Me, Harry Jenkins, who never wrote on anything he didn't swipe from a hotel lobby, suddenly had his name on a fancy letterhead. Me, who never had more than a couple of hundred bucks in his pocket, was suddenly throwing money around like there was no tomorrow. It was the longest drunk a man's ever been on—and not a drop of liquor, so to speak."

"What sobered you up?"

"Tomorrow," Jenkins said. "Tomorrow came. If it was the longest drunk, it sure as hell brought the biggest hangover. I won't be over it until I get out of this place."

"Where's B. J. now?"

"I don't know."

"Take a guess."

"I'm a lousy guesser. Look at my record."

"Try."

"I kind of guess he's dead."

"Why?"

"Some people make out okay in the Quarry but B. J. wasn't the type. First off, he was the wrong nationality. He kept demanding his rights and bail and habeas corpus and a bunch of stuff they never heard of in this country and wouldn't care if they had. Second off, he was a rich boy, spoiled rotten. He never had anything but the best all his life, and suddenly there he was with nothing but the worst. There we *both* were, only with me it didn't matter so much. If sheepshead is all they give me to eat—hell, I eat it. B. J. threw up just looking at it. Oversensitive he was, and then some. Bled like a stuck pig if he got the slightest scratch. And scratch he did, laddie, scratch he did. The mosquitoes had a banquet on him every night. You could hear them flying around laughing as soon as the sun went down. Call it buzzing, humming, hissing, whatever. Down here they laugh." He added with a touch of nostalgia, "One thing you could say about Jenlock Haciendas, we never had any mosquitoes there."

"Why not?"

"No water. Tons of sea water but no drink water."

"You should have thought of that before you started thinking of building a bunch of haciendas."

"Oh, we did. B. J. said it was no problem. All we had to do was build a desalinization plant to take the salt out of the sea water. He put up the money, and I mean large money. He wanted the best. Me, I never heard of a desalinization plant before, but by God, suddenly there I was with the wherewithal, so I started building one. You know what I'd do if I had it to do all over again, laddie?"

"Tell me."

"I'd take every penny and lam out of there. Nasty, you say? Not a bit of it. I would have been doing both of us a favor, like putting a plug in a sink where a heap of money was going down the drain. Down the drain, that's how it was. Before you could say 'desalinization,' things began going wrong. The boom started and the price of everything doubled, tripled, quadrupled. Supplies had to come by boat, and mostly they didn't. Work crews had to be trucked in, and so did water. Maybe one arrived, maybe the other, maybe neither. And all the time the government was making up new rules about building on the coast. Boy, I wouldn't go through that again for a million dollars." He added wistfully, "Which is roughly what I expected to make."

"That much."

"I told you, I was drunk, crazy drunk, without touching a drop. Well, at least I didn't lose much except time. B. J. lost everything, shirt, pants and shoelaces. Funny about that man. He must have been over fifty then, but I swear he was like a five-year-old kid believing in everything, Santa Claus, the Easter bunny, the tooth fairy."

"I don't see you as a tooth fairy, Jenkins, though you'd be pretty good at extractions."

Jenkins made a small sound like a mosquito's laugh. "So I didn't fit the role. Well, I never asked for it, either. I got sucked into somebody else's dream. B. J. really *believed* in Jenlock Haciendas. In his mind's eye the whole project was built and operating, the haciendas occupied, people playing on the golf course, swimming in the pool, sailing around the marina, even flushing their toilets. Sure, they sent both of us to jail for fraud, but with B. J. there actually was no fraud, just a big fat dumb dream . . . Well, that's all over now and good riddance." For the first time since he entered the room, Jenkins' eyes brightened. "I've been thinking, if I could lay my hands on enough cash, I'd open up a fried chicken business here. Quality stuff only, both table and takeout service."

"I don't think you have the beard for it, Jenkins."

"You may be missing out on a fortune. Mexicans are crazy about chicken and if we coated it with corn meal it would be sort of like a chicken tortilla. Roll that around on your tongue. Savor it. How does it taste?"

"It tastes like one of the residents of Jenlock Haciendas just tried to flush his toilet."

"Hell, you probably don't have the money, anyway. That's a cheap suit you're wearing."

"J. C. Penney's."

"You got to think bigger than J. C. Penney's, laddie. With a well-tailored suit you could make a pretty good appearance, sort of the ambitious but honest type."

"Thanks. I'll try it someday."

"Nothing too extreme, remember. People distrust extremities. One of my own weaknesses was Hawaiian shirts. I should have known better. Who's going to trust a man in a Hawaiian shirt with anything but a ukulele concession? Nobody. Not even B. J."

"Would you like another beer?"

"I better be moseying along to the Domino Club or El Alegre. This is the best time of night for new contacts."

"Suckers."

Jenkins shrugged. "Same difference. I got to live, don't I? And if the tourists didn't have money to spare they wouldn't be here, so it's not like robbing orphans and widows ... Oh hell, let the suckers wait. One more beer would be nice considering how we're down to brass tacks, you and me. I don't often get to the brass-tacks stage with people. I hope it doesn't become a habit."

"I don't think you have to worry."

The third beer increased Jenkins' spirit of camaraderie. "Laddie me lad, what do you want to know? Name it. What's mine is yours—for a small stipend, of course."

"So you think B. J. died in jail."

"He was a sick man, I told you. Cried a lot, couldn't eat, shriveled up like a prune. The guards kept him pretty well doped so he'd be quiet and wouldn't bother anyone."

"Suppose he didn't die but simply served his time and was released. Where would he be likely to go?"

"If he didn't have a habit, back to Bahía de Ballenas, maybe. Only he had a habit, a big one. You can't feed a habit by holing up in a little Mexican village. You got to get out and fight, hustle, beg, steal. Poor B. J. He was soft as a marshmallow; none of that would come natural to him."

"Perhaps he had someone who'd do it for him."

"You mean Tula?"

"It's possible, isn't it?"

"Oh, she could do it, all right. She was hustling a couple of weeks after she hit town. But I doubt that a nickel of the money she picked up went to B. J. She was a taker, not a giver."

"Why do you say *was?*"

"I don't know whether she *is* or not. So to me she's *was* until I find out for sure."

"Can you find out?"

"Maybe. I never tried. Me and Tula weren't real buddy-buddy. Know what she used to call me? Uncle Harry. Me, half a dozen years younger than her husband and still in the prime, so to speak."

"What was her attitude toward B. J.?"

"As long as the money held out, she put on a show of affection. She even came to see him in jail a few times for what they call in polite society 'connubial privileges.' That's probably where she got the idea of taking up the work professionally. On visiting days the hustlers flock around the jail like starlings. Tula just naturally followed the flock. There wasn't much else she was prepared to do, she couldn't read or write. I used to see her once in a while, all gussied up hanging around the cheap bars. She pretended not to recognize me. Good old Uncle Harry found himself de-uncled."

"You don't think she might have paid B. J.'s fine, or put up bail or bribe money?"

"Not in a million years would be my guess. But what's that worth? Women are not reasonable creatures, so how can a reasonable man like me tell what they're going to do?"

"Let's assume," Aragon said, "that Tula is still in town and you have the right connections for finding her."

"Consider it assumed. And then?"

"I'd like to ask her some questions. Given enough time, I might be able to find her myself. But I don't know the city, what name she's using, where her hangouts are, or even what she looks like."

"So how much is it worth to you if I ask around?"

"Two hundred dollars."

Jenkins ran an expert eye up and down the J. C. Penney suit, the Sears, Roebuck shirt and the orange birthday tie from his cousin Sandoval, who was color-blind.

"You can't afford that kind of money, laddie, unless the job is real important. Two hundred is pretty small potatoes for something real important. Let's raise the ante to three hundred, fifty in advance."

The deal was settled at $250. Gilly might squawk, but Aragon had the feeling that if she and Jenkins ever met, at the Domino Club or El Alegre, they would understand each other immediately.

Jenkins put the bills Aragon gave him in his coat pocket. "I could walk out of here with this fifty and you might never see me again. Did that occur to you?"

"Certainly. You won't do it, though. You need the rest of the money to help you get out of town. There's Emilia and the turnip mashing, remember?"

"Hell, how could I forget. One of those relatives of hers is probably standing right outside the hotel this very minute waiting for me to come out. It's not fair. Me, I don't have a relative in the world unless it's a kid some place where I got careless . . . Did you know B. J. and Tula had a kid?"

"I've heard of him."

"Crazy as a coot. Makes funny noises."

"We all make funny noises. Some may be just a little funnier."

"Is that philosophy or bullshit, laddie?"

"A little of both."

"No matter. I try to avoid stepping in either." Jenkins stood up. He was unsteady on his feet, and small round patches of red had appeared at the tip of his nose and on both cheekbones like the make-up of a circus clown. "I'd better start to work. That two fifty ought to set me up in Mexicali. Mexicali's full of tourists, it'll be a gold mine."

"Stay out of real estate."

"Oh, I can't truly regret Jenlock Haciendas. It was a great place while it lasted." It sounded like a fitting epitaph.

Aragon said, "Suppose you come back here tomorrow night and give me a progress report."

"If that's how you want it."

"I'll be waiting for you. Good night, Jenkins."

"I have a nice feeling about you, laddie. You're going to bring me luck."

Eleven

Twenty-four hours later Aragon was still waiting in his hotel room to hear from Harry Jenkins. It was after eleven when the phone finally rang.

"It's me, laddie."

"Where are you?"

"Never mind about that. Listen, I said you were going to bring me luck, and by God, you did. I met this pigeon. He came down to Mexico to scout around for investment opportunities and I happen to have one for him. Me."

"I've already invested in you, fifty bucks, two hundred more coming. I'm expecting a report."

"All in good time. This other matter is more urgent. The pigeon's due to leave town pretty soon and I'm trying to nail him down."

"What are you nailing him to?"

"The chicken tortilla business. He thinks it's a winner."

"How many drinks has he had?"

"That's not a nice implication," Jenkins said reproachfully. "But I won't hold a grudge. Maybe you got something against chickens, maybe you just lack financial vision."

"Did you find Tula?"

"I'm on her heels. By tomorrow night I'll be able to take you straight to her."

"Why not tonight?"

"I told you, tonight I'm involved in a new business venture."

"Where are you?"

"Now, why do you want to know that?"

"Because wherever it is, I'm coming. I want to protect my investment."

"Oh hell, laddie, don't do that. You'll blow it for me. This may be my chance of a lifetime. He's fat and juicy and ready for plucking."

"Let's get back to Tula."

"Sure, sure, whatever you say. Only I'm in kind of a hurry."

"I think you're bulling me," Aragon said. "You already know where the girl is, don't you?"

"Even if I told you, you couldn't find her. It's not like she has an ordinary job with a real address and maybe even a telephone. Looking for customers while dodging the police, that takes moving around, see?"

"Where are you, Jenkins?"

"I asked you not to press me, laddie," Jenkins said and hung up.

Aragon put the phone back on the hook. It was late and he was tired. He would have liked to go to bed and forget about Jenkins for the night, but the conversation had made him uneasy on two counts. The first was the possibility that if Jenkins plucked enough feathers out of his new pigeon, he wouldn't wait around town for Gilly's extra two hundred. He'd be in Mexicali by morning.

The second possibility was in a sense more disturbing. Rich, drunk, gullible tourists were not uncommon in Rio Seco, but the fact that Jenkins found one so quickly and easily was suspicious. Nobody was easier to con than a con man, and Jenkins would be easier than most. He seemed to have the same kind of basic innocence he'd criticized in B. J. If B. J. believed in Santa Claus and the tooth fairy, Jenkins believed in rainbows with pots of gold. The only thing that would protect him from being taken was that he had nothing much to take, only the fifty dollars he'd received in advance for locating Tula.

Aragon was almost certain that Jenkins had found out where the girl lived and that the reason he'd refused to give more information over the phone was his fear of not being paid the extra two hundred. For someone in Jenkins' position it was a natural enough fear. He'd probably cheated and been cheated hundreds of times. Now that he had something real to sell he would deliver it in person, for cash and in his own time. Meanwhile, some half-soused American tourist was hearing a lot about chicken tortillas.

As he put on his coat and tie Aragon thought back over the conversation. Jenkins had not, in fact, mentioned the word "American," only a pigeon ready for plucking. The pigeon could be an Eskimo or an Algerian, but the odds were against it. Emilia had named three places as Jenkins' favorite hangouts because they catered to American tourists, and Jenkins had referred to two of them the previous night, El Alegre and the Domino Club.

Aragon combed his hair and straightened his tie in front of the bureau mirror. "You're going out on the town, laddie."

El Alegre was in a new section of town that was already beginning to look old and in another few years would be just another addition to the slums. Right now business was booming. A fleet of taxicabs was double-parked outside the entrance vying with each other for the attention of the hustlers. Jenkins had compared the girls hanging around outside the jail to a flock of starlings. That was how they looked now as they gathered on the sidewalk in front of the club, like starlings getting ready to roost for the night, twittering, fluttering, fidgeting, grumbling.

A teenager wearing a high-rise platinum wig and four-inch cork wedgies attached herself to Aragon's coat sleeve and spoke to him in English. "Hey, gringo, you and me make fun. What kind of fun? You name it. You tiger, me pussycat, me tiger, you pussycat."

"I'm here on business."

"Okey-dokey, we do business."

"No thank you."

"No okey-dokey?"

"No okey-dokey."

"Son a bitch cheapskate." She returned to the flock, twitching her tail and smoothing her ruffled feathers. She was about fifteen, the age Tula had been when she'd gone to work as a maid in Gilly's house.

Aragon looked over the girl's companions, wondering if Tula

was one of them. No, they were all too young. Tula would be twenty-three by now, young by the standards of an ordinary middle-class American, old for a prostitute in Rio Seco.

"Hey, gringo, lotsa fun. Play games. Hot stuff."

The Domino Club was on the other side of the bridge crossing the seasonally dry river that gave the city its name. It was October and the rainy season was late starting. The *rio* was *seco* after months of drought, just as the wells in the higher sections of the city were drying up and those nearer the sea were turning to salt.

In earlier days a narrow wooden bridge had divided the slums and squatters from the residential areas of the more prosperous merchants and professional men. With the building of the new bridge over the new concrete lining of the riverbed, the two sections of town were becoming indistinguishable. Thousands of cars and pedestrians crossed the steel arch every day. The wealthier citizens resented the intrusion and escaped to the hills and the privacy of iron gates and chain-link fences. Their deserted houses were torn down for apartments or rebuilt into stores or night clubs like the Domino.

Several coats of black paint decorated with white polka dots, a black-and-white marquee topped by a neon sign indicated that the Domino catered to a better class of clientele than El Alegre. A uniformed doorman kept the hustlers on the opposite side of the street, the taxicabs in single file and the cigarette butts swept into the gutter. Otherwise things were much the same, including the fact that Harry Jenkins wasn't in sight.

Aragon was on the point of leaving when he noticed a small man in a blue suit slumped over the table in the end booth. He thought of Emilia at the jail talking about Jenkins: *He's not a drunk, liquor's not one of his weaknesses.*

Tonight was the exception. Jenkins reeked of whiskey as though he'd spilled it all over himself. His head lay sideways on the table at an awkward angle looking detached from the rest of his body. Though his eyes were open, they were as unfocused and unblinking as a dead man's. One of his hands was curled around an empty bottle of beer.

"Jenkins? Hey, are you all right?"

Jenkins' mouth moved in response to his name, but the only

93

thing to come out of it were some bubbles of saliva that slid down his chin. Aragon took out his handkerchief and attempted to wipe off the saliva. Jenkins' whole face, his hair, his shirt and tie, even the shoulders of his suit coat were soaking wet. Instead of merely spilling some whiskey on himself, he seemed to have been the target of a whole glass of it, as though someone had thrown it at him in a rage.

"Jenkins, can you hear me?"

He moaned.

"What happened to you? Are you sick?"

One of the bartenders came over, a young man with a moist red face like underdone beef. He spoke English with a New York accent. "This a friend of yours?"

"I know him."

"That's good enough. Get him out of here. I don't want him puking up the place."

"I think he's sick."

"I don't care why he's doing it, just let him do it some other place."

"Help me lift him and I'll put him in a cab."

"I got a hernia."

"How can you have a hernia when you're all heart?"

"Just lucky, I guess. Use the back door."

Aragon managed to get his hands under Jenkins' armpits and pull him to his feet. "Come on, Jenkins, wake up. Wake up and see the birdie."

"Chicken birdie?"

"Chicken birdie it is. Can you walk?"

"I can *fly.*"

"Good. Let's fly home to roost."

Jenkins' eyes were coming back into focus. The pupils were so dilated that only a tiny rim of iris was left around them. He stood up, holding on to the table for support. "Who—are you?"

"I'm laddie. Remember?"

"Oh, I feel funny, laddie—help me, help."

"You'll be all right. Come along."

They walked arm in arm with a kind of awkward dignity out the back door and into a dimly lit area that had once been some-body's walled garden. A water-boy fountain, the pitcher on his shoulder long since dry, stood in the middle of dusty dying weeds. The only living relic of the garden was a half-naked tamarisk tree.

Aragon put the sick man down on the concrete bench that circled the fountain. Jenkins' forehead was hot and the pulse in his throat very rapid and irregular.

"Listen now, Jenkins. Wait here and I'll go line up a taxi and come back for you. Have you got that? I'm coming back for you, so *wait here.* Do you understand me?"

It was apparent even in the dim light that Jenkins was incapable of understanding. His eyes had glazed over, vomit was bubbling down both sides of his mouth, and he was alternately chewing and spitting out chunks of sentences. His symptoms didn't fit those of an ordinary drunk. He'd had a few moments of lucidity when his speech was clear and unslurred, and he recognized Aragon as a friend. Now he seemed to have slipped once again into a state of delirium.

"Big bird, fly me golden . . . help B. J., he's sick . . . must go home . . . takeout and delivery . . . fry me to the moon, Emilia . . . bad bird boy . . . where are you, laddie? Get me a drink. Water. *Water.*"

"I'm right here. I'm going away for a few minutes, then I'm coming back to take you home. Are you listening, Jenkins? You stay where you are. Don't move. I'm going for help."

"Where's laddie? Water. Drink."

Jenkins reached out and clutched the marble water boy with both hands. Aragon left him like that, hanging on to the statue as if it were still pouring out the stuff of life.

Aragon returned through the bar to the front of the building. He gave one of the taxi drivers waiting at the curb five dollars to come and help him with Jenkins. The two men were just starting toward the club when Jenkins himself came staggering out through the front door, his head lowered as if he were about to charge some unseen unknown enemy.

Aragon shouted at him, "Jenkins, wait for me. Hey, hold it!"

Jenkins turned and began running toward the bridge, dodging between pedestrians and around passing cars. He was small and agile, and whatever illness he was suffering from hadn't affected his speed. By the time he reached the bridge he was ahead of Aragon by a hundred yards or more. He started to cross the bridge, his arms flapping like the clipped wings of a chicken. Then, about a third of the way across, he suddenly stopped and clutched his stomach as though he was going to be sick again.

He leaned over the railing. People paid no attention to him. They were like travelers on the deck of a ship politely ignoring a fellow passenger who was seasick. Five seconds later he had disappeared into the concrete darkness below the bridge.

A woman screamed. A crowd gathered. People peered down into the darkness to see if anything exciting was going on. It wasn't. They walked on by.

Aragon stood at the railing. Beads of sweat rolled down his face, as cold and heavy as hail stones. *I have a nice feeling about you, laddie. You're going to bring me luck.*

"God Almighty," he whispered. "I'm sorry, Jenkins, I'm sorry."

A short fat young man stopped beside him. He wore a striped serape over his work clothes, and his hair was greased back over his head so that it looked like a black plastic cap. He had a wheezy worried voice: "Did you push him?"

"*Push* him? For Christ's sake, he was a friend of mine."

"Then why were you chasing him?"

"I was trying to help him."

"Why was he running away from you?"

"I don't know. Now will you please—"

"Pretty soon the police will arrive. Already I hear the sirens."

Aragon heard them too.

"They'll be nasty," the man said. "They always are when such a serious crime is committed."

"There was no crime."

"They arrest everyone in sight, helter-skelter. They have to act fast because corpses are usually buried the next day . . . What story will you give them?"

"No story. Just the truth. I was trying to save him, to take him home because he was sick."

"It didn't look that way to me. You were chasing him and he was trying to escape from you. The police don't like it when Americans come here to murder each other. It gives our country a bad reputation."

"Oh, for God's sake."

"And if the Americans also swear and blaspheme—"

"Okay, okay. How much?"

"Twenty dollars seems a small price to stay out of our jail. We have a very poor jail."

Aragon gave him a twenty-dollar bill and the man disappeared into the crowd as quickly as Jenkins had disappeared into the darkness below the bridge.

The sirens were getting closer. He started walking as fast as he could back toward the Domino Club. His legs felt rubbery and the sweat was still pouring down his face.

Twelve

The back booth at the Domino Club where Jenkins had been sitting was cleaned up and smelled of disinfectant. The cleanup even included the young bartender who'd spoken to him previously. He wore a freshly laundered white jacket with the name Mitchell stitched across the breast pocket.

Aragon sat down in the booth. About three minutes later Mitchell joined him, bringing along a cup of coffee. He didn't offer Aragon either the coffee or anything else.

"How's your friend?"

"Dead."

"Yeah? Well, when you gotta go, you gotta go."

"His name was Harry Jenkins," Aragon said quietly. "He wasn't a bad man, just unlucky. He had the wrong kind of friends."

"There's a right kind? Show me."

"What was he drinking?"

"Beer. I took the empty bottle away myself before I had one of the boys tidy the place up."

"Your boys are very thorough tidy-uppers. Do they always use a gallon of disinfectant after each customer?"

"The booth stank of puke and whiskey."

"You said Jenkins was drinking beer."

"I removed an empty beer bottle from this table. I didn't smell it to see what had been in it. I figured a beer bottle would contain beer. Anyway, that was his usual drink. He often came in and ordered a beer. He'd nurse a single bottle along for half the night, waiting around for a touch or whatever he had in mind. How come all this fuss over one little dead man?"

"I think he was poisoned."

"You think funny. Go home. Sleep it off."

Aragon looked at his watch. It was twenty after one. "Jenkins called me about two hours ago at my hotel. He was completely sober and in good spirits. Yet forty-five minutes and one bottle of beer later, he was so stoned out of his head that he went and jumped off a bridge. Does that make sense?"

"My business is to make money, not sense. And you know how I do it? I keep my nose clean and out of other people's affairs. I also stay away from booze."

"Jenkins told me on the phone that he was with somebody, an American."

"He wasn't an American."

"What was he?"

"Like I said, I mind my own affairs. But I couldn't help noticing that he was dark-skinned and wearing the usual Mexican work clothes, half native, half cowboy."

"How old was he?"

"They never show their age. I hired one last year, thought he was about thirty, until suddenly he dropped dead of old age. It's all that grease in their skin, keeps the wrinkles away."

"Did Jenkins and his companion seem friendly?"

"There was no quarrel, no fuss, no nothing, until you showed up."

"When I showed up, Jenkins was alone and you seemed pretty anxious to get rid of him."

"I hate pukers."

"You hate a lot of people, don't you, Mitchell?"

"In this business you see their worst side, until pretty soon you forget they have a better one. And ten chances to one they haven't, anyway. Any more questions?"

"What happened to Jenkins between the time he phoned me and the time I arrived?"

"Nothing happened to him. He got drunk, took a walk to

sober up, fell off a bridge. Period." Mitchell finished his coffee. "So don't throw any wild statements around. Our club has a good reputation, the best that money can buy. When a little trouble comes along, zap, it goes away again. The police are very understanding."

"How much are cops selling for these days?"

"They're dirt cheap. Which is what dirt ought to be, cheap."

"That's not much of a tribute to your protectors."

"I pay them, I don't have to kiss their asses," Mitchell said. "Now, if it will shut you up and make you feel any better, I'm sorry about your friend."

It was the first human remark Mitchell had made. "The coffee must be getting to you," Aragon said. "For a minute there I thought I heard the faint beating of a heart."

"I have the hiccups."

Aragon drove to the police station and waited around for the rest of the night. At seven in the morning he was informed that Jenkins' body had been examined, and death was declared the result of injuries received in an accidental fall. Fifty dollars was found in his pocket, enough for funeral expenses. In Rio Seco, funerals were cheap, since there was no embalming, and quick if there were no survivors to wait for and the weather was hot. The body was removed to an undertaking parlor, a priest was notified, and Jenkins' funeral service was scheduled for six o'clock that night.

Death was always sad, the undertaker told Aragon. "But one must be realistic. The new bridge is good for business. More than thirty people have already jumped from it."

"The police said Jenkins' death was accidental."

"Such a verdict makes it easier for them. Also for the Church. The Church frowns on suicide."

"I think Jenkins was drugged, which makes it murder not accident or suicide."

"Oh no, no no. The bridge is a magnet for troubled souls seeking oblivion or what not. You have one like it in San Francisco, the Golden Gate. I read in the newspaper that more than five hundred people have jumped from it. Is this true?"

"I don't know."

100

"Newspapers tell the truth, certainly?"

"When they recognize it and when they want to, like you and me. The truth about Jenkins is that he was murdered."

"God must decide such things," the undertaker said. "He is the Final Judge."

The funeral service was held in the cemetery in a mixture of Spanish and Latin, and Jenkins' name was pronounced Arry Yenkeen. The only other mourner was the fat young man in the striped serape who'd accosted Aragon on the bridge. When their eyes met across the open grave, he pretended not to recognize Aragon. But as soon as the service was over and the priest had departed, the man spoke: "We meet again."

"Yes. I hope it doesn't become a habit. I can't afford it."

"You mean the money?" He pulled a twenty-dollar bill out of his pocket. "I didn't want this for myself. It's for my sister, Emilia Ontiveros, to buy a mourning dress and to light candles. She is stricken with grief."

Aragon thought of the jailed woman with her scarred hands and arms and her despairing eyes. In a crude sense she was lucky: her grief would be less caustic this way than the way Jenkins had planned.

"It was a great love," Ontiveros said. "A little more so on her part, naturally, because he was a man and men meet more temptations. Harry was always meeting temptations, especially when Emilia wasn't around to head them off. Lighting candles for him is a waste of good money—he wasn't even a Catholic. But Emilia is beyond reason. She can't see how much better off she'll be with him gone. He roused her to terrible angers. Without these angers she'd be safe at home, leading a nice normal life."

"What did you tell her about this death?"

"That he drank too much, lost his balance and fell over the railing. She didn't believe it."

"Why not?"

"Harry didn't get drunk. In all their good and bad times together she never once saw him drunk. She told me that B. J. must have pushed Harry over the railing."

"Who is B. J.?"

"An American, somebody Harry knew in the old days. Harry

was responsible for him being sent to jail. B. J. swore he'd get even. Maybe it's true. I've never met this man, B. J., he may be very bad, very vengeful, but I can't always take Emilia's word for things. Her great passion makes fires in her mind and you can't poke around until the ashes cool." Ontiveros ran the back of his hand across his forehead as though he felt the sudden heat of one of Emilia's fires. "I'm the oldest son in the family. It's my duty to look after Emilia and maybe someday to find her a real husband. This will be easier with Harry gone."

It was getting late. No workmen had appeared to fill in the grave, as though they were in no hurry to appear for such a cheap funeral of such an unimportant man.

"You were on the bridge," Aragon said. "You saw what happened."

"Not everything. It was night and there were many people. One of them could have been B. J. It wouldn't have been hard to do. Harry was a small man and not a worker in strong condition like myself—he would need only a little push, so quick, so natural."

Aragon stared down into the open grave with its plain pine box. Had B. J. long since been put into one like it? Or could he still be alive and here in Rio Seco? Suppose he'd found out that Gilly was looking for him. Suppose he wanted to avoid her as much as Harry Jenkins had wanted to avoid Emilia.

"For all I know," Ontiveros said, "*you* might be B. J."

"No, I'm looking for him."

"Why?"

"His wife would like to see him again."

"She has great passion like Emilia?"

"She had at one time."

"And fires in the mind?"

"Yes, I think so."

"Such women are a nuisance. Day in, day out, the family nags at me to find Emilia a husband. I might be able to do it finally now that Harry's gone. If I had some way of collecting a little money for her dowry—"

"No."

"No?"

"No."

"Then I might as well be going." Ontiveros picked up a handful of earth, threw it on top of the coffin and crossed himself. "That's from Emilia."

He walked away, his serape flapping around his knees.

The sun was setting, expanding into an improbably brilliant flame-red ball. It looked like one of the fires in Emilia's mind. Or Gilly's. In ten minutes it had fallen into ashes below the horizon.

Thirteen

He called Gilly that night after dinner. He had nothing better to tell her this time than last time, so he poured himself a double Scotch before he tried to contact her. He got his message across in a hurry: Jenkins was dead and buried, Tula still missing, and the search for B. J. had come to a halt.

Her reaction was unexpected—no shock, no anger. She merely sounded depressed. "We've lost."

"Yes."

"You might as well come home."

"All right."

There was a long silence, then a sudden burst of words. "I can't—I *can't* let it go like this. I can't leave him in a dreary foreign prison."

He didn't say what he thought: *You could and you did, Gilly. Your grief may be genuine but it's years too late, miles too short.*

She said, "Jenkins at least had a decent burial, yet it was all his fault. He dragged B. J. down into the gutter."

"B. J. dragged easy, Mrs. Decker. Let's call it a *folie à deux.* Neither man would have gotten into such a crazy predicament without the other."

"You've turned against B. J. Jenkins won you over."

"Let's not make this a personal thing, Mrs. Decker."

"It's personal to *me*. Not to you, naturally. I never met a lawyer yet who had any more feeling than a dead mackerel."

Gilly was returning to normal.

"And you can quote me to that pompous old boss of yours, Smedler. Tell him the whole damn Bar Association hasn't enough heart for a single baboon."

"He won't be surprised," Aragon said. "Now that your opinion of lawyers has been clarified, I'll continue my report."

"Why did you let Jenkins get away from you?"

"That's not quite accurate, Mrs. Decker. When he refused to tell me over the phone where Tula was, I went after him and found him. But someone else got to him first and slipped something into the bottle of beer he was drinking. Whether it was intended to kill him, I don't know."

"Something like what?"

"I don't know that either."

"And why?"

"A possible motive might have been to prevent him from giving out any more information, either about B. J. or about Tula."

"Maybe it was a simple robbery."

"He had fifty dollars on him when he was found, enough for his funeral. It was your fifty, by the way."

"So the funeral was my treat." She let out a small brittle laugh. "If life is funny, how about death? It's a real scream."

"It was for Jenkins. He screamed all the way down."

Another silence. "Why do—why do you tell me things like that?"

"Because I'm a lawyer, I like to make people feel rotten."

"You're an extremely unpleasant young man."

"Right now I'm not so crazy about you either. And I'm damn glad I'm through working for you."

"What makes you think you're through working for me?"

"You said I was to come home."

"So I did. But at the moment—between insults—you're still on the job, giving me your report. You may continue."

Aragon swallowed a chunk of pride, washing it down with a second glass of Scotch. "When Jenkins called me here late last night he was pretty high, not on drugs or alcohol, on hope and anticipation. He said he had a pigeon. I don't think so. I think he

105

was the pigeon. The only description I could get of his companion was that he was wearing the clothes of an ordinary Mexican workingman. This doesn't jibe with what Jenkins told me, that the meeting offered him the chance of a lifetime, that his so-called pigeon had come down to Mexico—note the word 'down'—to scout around for investment opportunities and that he was ready to put money into the chicken tortilla business which Jenkins was touting. We're faced with quite a few contradictions if we look at Jenkins' death from only one viewpoint."

"I have only one viewpoint," Gilly said. "My own."

"I'm aware of that, Mrs. Decker. But others do exist. Jenkins had a pretty shady past and he's undoubtedly been involved in dozens of scams in the past couple of years. That was the way he lived. Maybe it was the way he died, and B. J. and Tula and you and I had nothing to do with it."

"Naturally, I like the idea. I don't want a man's death on my conscience if I can help it."

"Let's leave it at that, then. Jenkins had other enemies."

"What do you mean by other?"

"Other than B. J."

"B. J. wasn't his enemy. That was the trouble—he should have been. B. J. was nobody's enemy."

Emilia has a different idea, Aragon thought. But she's in jail and crazy with grief and crazy without it. Nobody will believe her. Except me, dammit. Except me.

"Tell me about the girl, Tula," Gilly said. "Though she isn't a girl any more, is she? That's some consolation, I guess."

"When B. J. was arrested she followed him to Rio Seco."

"How touchingly faithful."

"Not exactly. She went into business for herself."

"What kind of business, a taco stand or something?"

"She's a hooker."

Her little gasp of surprise sounded genuine. "I—I'm sorry. I didn't expect—I didn't want that kind of fate for her."

"People's fates don't depend on what you want, Mrs. Decker, not even your own."

"I wish you'd have something nice to tell me for once instead of all this ugliness and death and dirt."

"You gave me a dirty job," Aragon said. "I'm glad it's over."

"Wait a minute, don't hang up. Reed's here trying to—*I wish you'd stop interrupting, I can't listen to two people at once. All right, I'll ask him*—Reed wants to know if you've been to the American consulate."

"No."

"They often get information about American citizens which the Mexican authorities don't have or won't admit having. Reed thinks you should go there and ask questions before you come home."

"It's a good idea."

"Will you do it?"

"Yes."

"That means you're still working for me?"

"I guess I am."

"Try sounding a little happier about it."

"Yippee," Aragon said and hung up.

Ordinarily it was Reed who put Marco to bed after dinner. Tonight Gilly did it herself. She gave him a sponge bath, then she rubbed his back with alcohol and dusted it with baby powder. She cleaned his teeth and applied moisturizing cream to his lips and drops to lubricate the eye that never closed. She gave him his shots, one to help him sleep, another to keep him free of pain for a few hours. She wasn't as quick or thorough as Reed and she did some things the hard way, like the bath in the wheelchair instead of on a rubber sheet on the bed. But in the end everything was done and Gilly had a real sense of accomplishment. She'd always been full of natural energy and it was a relief to use some of the surplus on a constructive task.

Violet Smith came to say good night before she left for her evening meeting at the church of the Holy Sabbathians. She assisted Gilly in lifting Marco out of his chair and into the bed. He was very light and brittle, like a hollow glass child.

"Upsy-daisy," Violet Smith said cheerfully. "My stars, he's getting skinny. It casts a reflection on my cooking."

"Why shouldn't it?" Gilly said. "You're not a very good cook."

"I never claimed I was. Anyway, *cordon bleu* would be wasted in this house, what with sickness and booze and that fancy-pantsy male nurse who thinks he's Mr. Wonderful. I do good plain cooking for good plain folks." She emphasized the word "good." It might not help, but it certainly wouldn't hurt. "Nighty-night, Mr. Decker. We'll all be praying for you at the meeting."

Gilly waited until Violet Smith was out of earshot. "Reed thinks we should try and stop her from going to these meetings. He doesn't trust her discretion. What do you think?"

She often asked his opinion to make him feel he had a hand in running the house. She even waited a few seconds after each question as though giving him a chance to consider and to answer. He had no answer. If he had, he couldn't have spoken it, and if he could have spoken, he wouldn't. Answers were useless when there were no issues left to be resolved, only time to be put in.

"She and Reed are beginning to feud over everything. Someday when you're better I'll fire both of them, and you and I will take a long trip together. Maybe I'll buy another home on wheels like Dreamboat . . . Just think, if B. J. and I had gone away together in Dreamboat the way I'd planned, none of these terrible things would have happened. He wouldn't have deserted me for Tula and wouldn't have gotten involved with Harry Jenkins and been sent to jail. Tula wouldn't be walking the streets in Rio Seco, and Jenkins himself would be alive. You've often heard me talk about Jenkins, B. J.'s old partner in crime."

She watched the fingers of his right hand to see if he raised them to indicate interest. They didn't move. Perhaps the sleeping hypo had already taken effect; perhaps he couldn't remember Jenkins and didn't want to. She went on talking anyway. Nothing could have stopped her now.

"Jenkins died last night and was buried late this afternoon. They bury people as soon as possible in Mexico, I'm not sure why. The funeral only cost fifty dollars, imagine that. In this town they don't even allow you to look at a coffin for fifty dollars. Since he's already buried, there won't be an autopsy and probably nobody will ever know for sure what killed him. Aragon thinks some kind of drug was slipped into his drink. He didn't say so directly but he gave the impression that he suspects B. J. did it. That's rather funny, isn't it?"

He didn't think it was funny. Laughter had been lost longer and farther back in his brain than speech.

"Naturally, I told Aragon the idea was ridiculous. I'm not so sure it was, though. Oh, I know B. J. could never have done anything *violent*. But merely putting something in a drink, that's such a quiet little crime, hardly more than running off with one of the servants."

He willed her to stop talking and go away. It was useless. His will had no more power than the rest of him. He could only listen and wish he was deaf and hope for an earthquake, a thunderstorm, the ringing of a phone, a dog barking, the sound of a car in the driveway, a low-flying plane. *Shut up and leave me alone, leave me be.*

"And Tula," she said. "Poor little Tula. I drove down to Rio Seco years ago before B. J. and I were married. It was an evil place. You could smell it rotting, the garbage, the sewage in the streets, the decadence and decay. What a strange fate for such a pretty young girl. A 'nymphet' I believe they'd call her nowadays. You know what a nymphet is? I looked it up in the encyclopedia. It's a young nymph. And a nymph is like a larva and a larva is sort of a worm. Wormlet—that doesn't sound quite so flattering or mysterious, does it? Wormlet. It describes her perfectly." Her brief laugh was more like a cough. "If the worm turns, I wonder if the wormlet makes a turnlet. B. J. would have thought that was funny. He had a nice sense of humor."

I don't. Go away.

She pulled the woolen blanket up around his shoulders. "B. J.'s women, Ethel, me, Tula—they're the only ones I know of for sure—none of us have had happy lives. I'm not claiming it was his fault, it's just a fact. Maybe he wrecked things for people, maybe he chose people who were bound to wreck things for themselves. Anyway, Tula's life is finished and Ethel has lost herself in some weird religious group. That leaves me. I might still have a chance . . . Yes, the more I think about it, the more the idea appeals to me of buying another motor home like Dreamboat. I won't be able to get one exactly like it because that was eight years ago, they've probably changed quite a few things about it. But basically it will be Dreamboat, and I'll have the name painted on it just the same way. Then when you're better, you and I will go on a vacation together."

She smiled down at him. It was a stage smile that, seen at a distance, might have projected warmth and good cheer. Close up, it chilled him. Her mouth was cold red wax, her teeth were dwarf tombstones, the dimple in her cheek was a hole made by an icepick.

"You and I, dearest," she said, "you and I will go on a long vacation."

It was the night Ethel Lockwood was scheduled to address her fellow Sabbathians. The group leader for the occasion had been a poor choice, a nervous young man who stammered and was attempting to overcome his affliction by making protracted speeches in public.

"And so in c-c-conclusion, let me w-w-welcome our f-f-f-friend in need and our f-f-f-friend in deed, Ethel."

"Thank you, George," Ethel said, wishing they hadn't picked such an incompetent boob to introduce her, "for the long long long introduction."

It was too late now for her to read the pages of blank verse she'd written as a tribute to the Holy Sabbathians and their evenings of cleansing and healing. It would have been a shame to omit any of it, so she decided to save it for next time. Sin and sickness were very dependable: there would always be a next time.

Ethel's outfit had been purchased for the occasion at a thrift-shop. The ivory-colored chiffon dress looked gauzy and spiritual and floated around her like ectoplasm.

"Thank you also, sisters and brothers, for giving me this opportunity." To match her dress she wore her best voice, so delicate it seemed to emanate from another world.

"Speak up, I can't hear you," Violet Smith said from the back row.

"I came here this evening not for myself but for the sake of a very ill and helpless man. He is at the mercy of a merciless woman. I have known her for many years and I repeat, she is without mercy. I beg the Lord to intercede on his behalf."

"Wh-wh-what is the p-p-p-problem, sister?"

"I wish you wouldn't interrupt me any further, George. I am about to state the problem. This woman I referred to has engaged a man to find her first husband. If and when he is found, I have reason to believe that the second husband, the sick man, will be— I hesitate to say such a word, to think such a thought, but even the

110

most devout Christian must sometimes entertain unchristian thoughts."

"Entertain" seemed exactly the right word. The audience stirred in anticipation. Ethel's previous confessions had been dull and her illnesses commonplace: eating red meat, loss of temper, sinusitis and impacted wisdom teeth.

"What I'm afraid of," Ethel said, "is that this poor old man will be murdered."

She went on speaking. Every now and then she raised her arms, and from her angel-wing sleeves would come the scent of gardenias to sweeten the poisoned air.

"Violet Smith is late getting home tonight," Gilly said. "It must be a very interesting meeting."

Fourteen

It was almost midnight when Aragon's call to his wife in San Francisco was finally put through. Once the connection to the hospital was made, he had to hang on the line for another five minutes while Laurie was tracked down and brought to a phone.

She sounded breathless. "Hello, Tom?"

"How did you know it was me?"

"The operator told me. She recognized your voice. She thinks it's cute."

"Well?"

"Well what?"

"What do you think?"

"You roll your *r*'s a bit too much."

"Rrrrreally?"

"I don't mind. I roll mine too, being Scottish."

"Let's roll our *r*'s together."

"That sounds dirty," Laurie said. "I'm sure you didn't mean it that way."

"Are you."

"Well, sort of sure. Tom, have you been drinking?"

"Just enough to ease the pain of reporting in to Gilly, the Dragon Lady."

"Is she that bad?"

"I don't know. And the more I talk to her, the more I don't know."

"You *have* been drinking. In fact, it sounds as if you're at a party. Are you?"

"I may be the only person in Rio Seco who isn't," Aragon said. "This is when all the natives start whooping it up. Men, women, children, dogs, donkeys, anything that can move is out moving."

"Would you like to be whooping it up with them?"

"No. I prefer to sit and talk to my beautiful wife who rolls her *r*'s."

"I think you're a dirty young man."

"You should know, lassie."

"That's the first time you've ever called me lassie," she said. "You sound sort of funny, Tom. What's the matter?"

"It's a long story, involving someone I liked ... I have a medical question to ask you. Can you spare a minute?"

"Ten or so. I'm on my break, in the interns' lounge."

"What do you know about hallucinogenic drugs?"

"More than I want to, in one way. Not enough, in another. We've had kids brought in here so stoned we thought they were hopeless mental cases until the stuff wore off. Sometimes it didn't. Last month an eight-year-old boy died of respiratory failure after an overdose of mescaline. He was never able to tell us how much he took or where he got it. His parents are both users, involved in some kind of consciousness-raising meditation, but neither of them would admit anything. In fact, they threatened to sue the hospital ... Exactly what do you want me to tell you?"

"Just keep talking."

"The trouble is that so many new hallucinogens are available now in addition to old stand-bys like hashish and LSD. Their street names are often enticing—Cherry Velvet, Angel Dust, China Dolls. The lethal doses vary tremendously and there is no real antidote. If the victims are in a state of great excitement, we calm them down with tranquilizers or barbituric acid derivatives, or pump their stomachs if there's a chance some of the drug hasn't been absorbed into the system. Ordinarily, though, we simply provide custodial care until the effects wear off. Does this sound like a lecture?"

"I asked for it. Go on."

"In addition to the new drugs, we're faced with combinations of old ones, or mixtures of old and new, which can be lethal. A tolerable amount of cocaine taken at the same time as a tolerable amount of methedrine becomes intolerable . . . This someone you liked, is he dead?"

"He was killed in a fall from a bridge. The police claim it was an accident. In a broad sense they're right. If someone tampered with the brakes of my car and I couldn't stop in time to avoid a collision with a truck, it would be an accident. I think someone tampered with Jenkins' brakes. About forty-five minutes before I found him, he called me from a night club to postpone a date we'd made. He said he'd met someone with money to invest in Mexico and that he'd sold him the idea of investing in a chicken tortilla business. I was skeptical. I knew Jenkins was anxious to leave town before his girl friend got out of jail and I didn't want him to leave until he gave me the rest of the information he'd promised me. I went to the night club and found Jenkins in pretty bad shape. He was vomiting, sweating profusely and breathing very rapidly. He seemed to be out of his head. Or rather, in and out, mainly out. He recognized me briefly and talked to me."

"Did he ask you for anything?"

"Help. He asked me for help and I couldn't—"

"I meant something specific, a drink of water, perhaps."

"He asked me for some water. He even tried to get some for himself out of a fountain. The fountain was dry."

"Go on."

"I went to find help for him," Aragon said. "I thought he'd stay there at the fountain until I came back. He didn't. He started running away when he saw me again as if he was trying to escape from an enemy. I ran after him. He was probably heading for home, he lived on the other side of the bridge. Well, he didn't make it. Suddenly he went to the railing, leaned over and fell."

"Did he seem dizzy?"

"Crazy, dizzy, how do you tell the difference?"

"Vertigo and disorientation are both signs of LSD poisoning. So are the other symptoms you mentioned—profuse sweating, very rapid pulse, nausea and vomiting, dryness of the mouth, dilation of the pupils. An autopsy might reveal traces of LSD in the urine."

114

"There won't be an autopsy. He's already buried. And the bottle he was drinking from is in a pile of rubbish with a hundred other bottles like it, and the man he was drinking with can't be identified, let alone questioned."

"Is your story the only evidence of foul play?"

"My story is not evidence. Even if it were, even if the police were certain that Jenkins was murdered, it wouldn't concern them much. He was unimportant, an ex-convict with no money and a warrant waiting for him in Albuquerque and maybe a dozen other places. He was low man on the totem pole. There was no way up, no way down. The only way was out, to grow wings and fly out."

I met this pigeon . . . the chicken tortilla business is a winner . . . the hustlers flock around the jail like starlings . . . I'm chicken birdie, I can fly. "He talked a lot about birds. I mean, they came naturally into his conversation more than into most people's. He may even have been trying to fly when he went off the bridge."

"That's not uncommon with LSD."

Aragon heard a faint tap-tap-tap on the line and he knew Laurie was drumming her fingers on the table or desk the way she did when something was bothering her and she was trying to straighten it out in her mind. He said, "Okay, what's the matter?"

"The man who gave Jenkins the LSD, or whatever, had no way of predicting that Jenkins would either attempt to fly or suffer an attack of vertigo just as he happened to be crossing a bridge. He was betting on a very very long shot. That's dumb."

"So we have a dumb murderer. They're not, as a class, noted for brains."

"Or else the bridge thing wasn't actually necessary and the man was sure Jenkins had already ingested a lethal dose. He could have been waiting around for Jenkins to pass out when you appeared at the club and scared him off. . . . You have to consider a third possibility, too."

"Such as?"

"There wasn't any murder or any murderer. A couple of guys were getting their kicks by mixing drinks and drugs, like the housewife taking her Valium with a glass of muscatel or the high school kid carrying a flask of vodka to wash down the rainbows he can buy in the hall for a quarter apiece. Alcohol is usually half of the lethal mixtures in the cases that come our way."

"Jenkins was drinking beer—"

"Mild, but still alcohol. Drink enough and you're drunk."

"—and only one bottle, according to the bartender. The man with him was someone Jenkins hoped to con out of enough money to get him to Mexicali. He needed all his wits about him. He wasn't likely, under the circumstances, to mess around with any drugs or to break his pattern of nursing along one beer for a whole evening."

"So where are we?"

"Nowhere," he said. "I'll be going back to Santa Felicia either tomorrow or Friday. The Dragon Lady has asked me to check the American consulate here for any record of her ex-husband. After that I'll head for home and forget all about Jenkins and bridges and B. J. and Tula, the whole enchilada."

"No, you won't."

"How do you know I won't?"

"You've always liked enchiladas."

"I can take them or leave them."

"You'd better leave this one," she said. "I mean that seriously, Tom. You should be in court handling a complicated tax case or somebody's nice messy divorce."

"This *is* somebody's messy divorce, or was at the beginning. Now it's something even messier, something weird, crazy. I'm getting bad vibes."

"I speak as a doctor—there's nothing you can do for bad vibes except walk away from their source. So start walking."

"Tomorrow. Friday at the latest. May I ask you one more question?"

"You will, anyway."

"Is LSD readily accessible?"

"Here in San Francisco you can practically buy it over the counter if you go to the right counter. In Mexico the whole drug situation is pretty murky. Officially, narcotics and hallucinogens are illegal. Yet it's well known that mescal buttons and high-grade marijuana are widely grown. Less well known is the fact that opium poppies are cultivated just as successfully as they are in Turkey. The heroin extracted from them is not white like the stuff grown in Turkey. It's a peculiar color, that's why they call it Mexican Brown. It's equally strong, and a hundred times more dangerous because it's so much easier to smuggle into the country. There are nearly two thousand miles of border, most of it unguarded . . . But I haven't really answered your question. Maybe I was just postponing admitting that I don't know how accessible LSD is in Rio Seco. My guess is, not very. It's a product of labs, not fields. An American like Jenkins would be more likely than a Mexican to know about it and buy it."

"Good."

"Why good?"

"It fits in with what I've thought since the beginning, that the man with Jenkins at the Domino Club was an American and the bartender's description of him was phony. I'd better go and pay another call on Mitchell. He plays bartender, but I'm pretty sure he's part owner of the club."

"It's terribly late. And if Mitchell lied before, why shouldn't he lie again? You can't choke the truth out of him."

"He was bribed. I'll rebribe him."

"Tom, I hate the idea of your mingling with people like that in a place like that."

"I grew up in a barrio with people like that. I didn't even know there were any other kinds until I reached high school."

"Don't give me any of that *macho* bull."

"Okay, cut out the maternal bit. Bargain?"

"Some bargain," she said. "You do what you want and I'm too far away to stop you."

"How would you stop me, fair means or foul?"

"Diseases aren't the only things you learn about in med school. Definitely foul."

"I'll take you up on that some time."

"Tom, listen—"

"Stop worrying about me. I haven't been in a fight for ten years. Or five, anyway. I promise to be sensible, cautious, alert, et cetera, et cetera, et cetera."

"It would have been more reassuring without all those et ceteras," she said coolly. "And if you bring up that barrio stuff once again, I'll scream."

"You can't. You'll scare your patients."

"There aren't any patients in here. Just a couple of interns so tired they wouldn't wake up if a bomb exploded."

"Anyway, thanks for the information about drugs. I truly appreciate it."

"How truly?"

"I'll bring you a present, a great big sombrero to hide all those brains of yours. Us *macho* men like dumb dames."

"Go back to your enchilada. I hope you get heartburn."

"I love you too."

It was one o'clock, the peak of the evening in the Domino Club district. Before going inside, Aragon stopped to talk to the hustlers waiting across the street. There were about half a dozen left by this time. Most of them merely looked blank when Aragon mentioned the name. Tula Lopez. Only one, a girl about seventeen, said she used to know a Tula years ago when she first went into the racket. The Tula she knew must be very old by now, maybe twenty-five, and surely Aragon wouldn't be interested in such a hag.

"I just want to talk to her about a family matter. Can you put out the word?"

"How much word?"

"Twenty dollars. My name is Aragon and I'm staying at the Hotel Castillo."

"Sure, okay."

"What's your name?"

"Blondie."

"Blondie?"

The girl had jet-black hair reaching to her waist. "Why do you look funny? Don't you like that name?"

"I like it fine."

"So do all the other men. They laugh, it makes them feel good, I don't know why. But they give me more money when they laugh and feel good. How about you?"

"We agreed on a price."

When she opened her purse to deposit the twenty-dollar bill Aragon gave her, he saw the gleam of a knife. Blondie wasn't taking any chances on a customer getting away without paying.

He went inside the club. Mitchell saw him coming. He wasn't happy about it: "I thought you left town."

"I stayed around to pick up some loose ends."

"Loose ends is what we got plenty of. Take your pick."

"You lied to me, Mitchell."

"I lie a lot," Mitchell said. "I took a course."

"How much were you paid?"

"What for? Who by?"

"The American with Jenkins last night. How much did he pay you to forget he was here?"

"Nobody has to pay me to forget. I took a course in that, too. It's called Elementary Survival. I recommend it to you."

"Maybe I could hire you as a tutor. What do you charge?"

"Don't waste your money. You'd flunk the first lesson, how not to ask questions. The second lesson's even harder—how to spot a rat fink, get rid of him and stay in business. Adios, amigo, nice knowing you. Don't hurry back."

Fifteen

The American consulate was located in one of the older sections of the city, the Colonia Maciza. The formidable stone building reminded Aragon of the Quarry and he soon discovered another similarity. The consul and the assistant consul, like the warden and his assistant, believed in long weekends. They had, he was told by a receptionist, gone on a deep-sea fishing trip and wouldn't return until Monday afternoon. Possibly Tuesday. If there was a storm at sea, Wednesday. If the boat sank, never.

The consul's executive secretary sat behind a large mahogany desk with a name plate identifying her as Miss Eckert. She was fat as a robin, and she held her head on one side as if she were listening for a worm. Aragon did his best to provide a substitute by giving her his card, Tomas Aragon, Attorney-at-Law, Smedler, Downs, Castleberg, McFee and Powell.

Miss Eckert put on a pair of steel-rimmed spectacles, glanced at the card and then dropped it quickly into the wastebasket as though she'd detected a lethal fungus somewhere between Smedler and Powell.

"Is this a confidential matter, Mr. Aragon?"

"Yes."

"Then close the door. A man has been hanging around the

corridor all week. I suspect he may be CIA. You're not by any chance CIA?"

"Now, would I tell you if I were?"

"I don't know. I've never asked anyone before."

"The answer is no. But I may be lying."

Miss Eckert was not amused. She leaned back in her chair with a little sigh. "I gather your business concerns an American citizen in Baja."

"He came to Baja eight years ago. I'm not certain he's still here or if he's still alive. His family would like to find out."

"Name, please?"

"Byron James Lockwood."

"Last reported address?"

"The Quarry."

"The Quarry. That's the penitentiary."

"Lockwood was arrested on a charge of fraud involving some real estate in Bahía de Ballenas. I wasn't allowed access to the files at the Quarry. I was assured, however, that they contain no record of Lockwood's arrest or release."

"Are you sure he was taken there?"

"Positive. His partner in the fraud, Harry Jenkins, served time with him. I talked to Jenkins on Monday and again on Tuesday. On Wednesday I attended his funeral."

"Was he sick?—I refer to Monday and Tuesday, of course."

"No."

"This is beginning to sound," Miss Eckert said carefully, "like the kind of thing I would rather not hear."

"Better listen anyway. Jenkins told me—and this was confirmed by someone still in the jail—that Lockwood was ill and frequently disturbed and the guards used drugs to keep him from making trouble. Maybe in the beginning they gave him something like paregoric or laudanum to quiet him, but he eventually became drug dependent. He was wearing quite a bit of expensive jewelry when he left Bahía de Ballenas. He probably used it to purchase narcotics from, or through, the guards at the jail."

"Narcotics?" The word brought Miss Eckert's chair upright with a squawk of dismay. "What kind of narcotics?"

"I'm not certain."

"Oh, I knew, I *knew* this was going to be a rotten day. My

horoscope said, stay home and attend to family affairs. I thought it couldn't apply to me because I don't have a family. I should have taken the advice. It meant me, all right—*me.*"

"What's your sign?"

"Scorpio."

"That's the sign of a person who always copes, no matter how difficult the situation."

"I thought Scorpios were supposed to be creative."

"When they're not coping, they're creative."

"If you're trying to be funny," Miss Eckert said, "I may as well warn you that I have a very poor sense of humor. Especially when certain subjects are brought up. Poppies. Back home in Bakersfield I used to love poppies. Here it's a dirty word, and of course, a different kind of poppy, or *Papaver somniferum.*"

"Why? I mean, why is it a dirty word?"

"We—meaning all the U.S. government employees in this country—are in quite a delicate position right now. There are diplomatic negotiations going on between the two governments. Our government is well aware that illegal poppy fields are sprouting up all over the Sierra Madre, particularly the slopes on the Pacific side. It wants them destroyed. The Mexican government has pledged its cooperation and has actually burned off a few of the fields. But we're asking for more widespread and more complete destruction, such as Army helicopters spraying the fields with herbicides. Certainly we know that something must be done quickly. The last samplings of heroin picked up in LA showed that all of it, one hundred percent, came from Mexico. And the last New York samplings were eighty-five percent Mexican. The stuff which is grown in Turkey and processed in Marseilles has been drawing everyone's attention, while the Mexican stuff has been taking over the market. It's processed in mobile labs around Culiacan, north of Mazatlan. Law enforcement officials refer to Culiacan as the new Marseilles. You see the problem?"

"Clearly."

"Now the question is, What do we do about it? Obviously we can't tell the Mexican government officials to spray the fields or else. We must ask. Politely. That's called negotiating."

"And while these negotiations are taking place you want to avoid any international incidents."

"Yes."

122

"Such as might be caused by a prominent American citizen becoming a narcotics addict while confined in a Mexican jail unfairly if not illegally."

Miss Eckert looked grim. "That's what we want to avoid. Exactly."

"So let's you and I do a little negotiating of our own."

"I would rather not."

"The Mexican government would rather not destroy the poppy fields, and the United States government would rather they did."

"Which government am I supposed to be?"

"Take your pick."

"Swiss."

"Ah, you *do* have a sense of humor, Miss Eckert. Swiss. Ha ha."

"Ha ha," Miss Eckert said. "What are your terms?"

"I'll keep quiet about Lockwood, and you use some of your consular clout to find out if and when he was released from jail. Somebody must have a record of him—the state or local police, the jail officials, the immigration department, the coroner. You can open doors that are closed to me. So you open doors, I shut my mouth." Aragon took another card from his wallet and printed on it the address of his office and the telephone number. "You can write to me here, or if you want to phone, leave a message for me any time. There's an answering service after business hours."

"The consul should *be* here instead of out chasing fish or whatever. I can't decide something like this alone."

"Scorpios usually make quick decisions."

"That's what you want, is it—a quick decision? All right, here it is. I'm not going to break down doors trying to find traces of some junkie."

"You're not negotiating, Miss Eckert."

"I don't have to," Miss Eckert said. "I'm Swiss."

He flew back to Santa Felicia that afternoon. He found his car at the airport where he'd left it, the hub caps and radio antenna still in place, the windows and tires undamaged. Even the battery was in working order: the engine turned over after only three attempts. He took all this as a good omen.

He picked up a quarter-pounder and fries at a McDonald's

near the airport and ate them on the way home. It was ten o'clock when he called Gilly's house.

Violet Smith answered. "Good evening. Praise the Lord."

"Praise the Lord."

"Who's this?"

"Tom Aragon."

"Oh. Wait till I get a pencil and paper. She's not here. I'm supposed to write down whatever you say."

"But I haven't anything that important to—"

"Okay, I'm ready. You can say something."

"Where is she?"

"*Where . . . is . . . she.*"

"You don't have to write that down, for Pete's sake. This is personal, between you and me, like 'How are you.' "

"*Asked . . . regarding . . . health.*"

"Knock it off. All you have to write down is that I'm back in town and I'll talk to her tomorrow morning. There's nothing further to report, anyway."

"You didn't find Mr. Lockwood?"

"No."

"I must admit that's a load off my mind."

"Why must you admit that?"

Violet Smith made a number of small peculiar noises that sounded as though she might be wrestling with her conscience. "I just better not speak too freely over the telephone. You never know who might be listening in."

"Who else is there to listen in?"

"A new nurse, for one, Mrs. Morrison. She was hired so Reed could take a couple of days off this week, and Mrs. Decker decided to keep her on for a while until Reed's disposition improves. She's a nasty old thing, all starch and steel, not a human bone in her body."

"If she's listening in, she's certainly getting an earful."

"It won't come as a surprise. I made my feelings toward her quite clear, especially after they gave her the guest room. It's the best room in the house, a view of the ocean, a Beautyrest mattress and a pink velvet chaise. Pink velvet, and her an ordinary nurse."

Aragon said, "Where did Mrs. Decker go?"

"To the movies with Reed. Reed told her if she didn't get out of this house once in a while, she'd have a nervous breakdown. I felt like saying, maybe she already has one. But I didn't. My car's not paid for and my left back molar needs a new crown. There are also spiritual considerations."

"What kind of spiritual considerations?"

"The church needs money. Did you hear a click on the line just then?"

"I accidentally touched the phone with my glass."

"Your glass. What are you drinking?"

He lied a little. "Soda water."

"Reed has been drinking hard liquor lately, and far too much of it. His eyes get all bleary and he talks fresh to Mrs. Decker. If *I* talked fresh to her with bleary eyes, *I* wouldn't get away with it, no sir. She'd up and—"

"Violet Smith."

"—fire me like a shot. She allows Reed to—"

"Violet Smith, I'm tired. I want to go to bed."

"What time is it?"

"A quarter after ten."

"Went ... to ... bed ... ten-fifteen."

Sixteen

"Well, here he is, our wandering boy, fresh from foreign soil." Charity Nelson pushed back her orange wig so she could get a better view of him. "You've only been gone a week but I detect a certain new maturity about you, Aragon. What happened?"

"Nothing much."

"Did you miss me?"

"I thought of you a few times."

"I thought of you, too. Especially when the answering service woke me up at six-thirty this morning to read me a night letter addressed to you."

"A night letter?"

"From Rio Seco. Want me to read it to you? Better say yes, I took it down in my own version of shorthand."

"Yes."

"Please."

"Please."

"Please. Hasn't that word got a nice ring to it? I can't recall ever hearing it around this office before."

"You've put a very funny act together, Miss Nelson."

"There's more."

"Spare me. Double please."

"Okay." She consulted a piece of paper which she took from the top drawer of her desk. "It's signed 'Scorpio.' That sounds like a code name. In fact, the whole thing sounds as though it might be in code. You're not a spy, are you?"

"Yes."

"No kidding. Whose side are you on?"

"What sides are there? Pick one and read the letter."

" 'Swiss connection reports penetrating paper doors at the stone quarry'—I think that's what the operator said, 'stone quarry.' Does that make sense?"

"Yes."

" 'Records indicate Byron James Lockwood was released three years ago by Magistrate Guadalupe Hernandez. Exact circumstances of Lockwood's release unavailable and current whereabouts unknown. Hernandez contacted by phone but refused to give additional information. Home address, Camino de la Cima. Try Mordida.' Who's Mordida?"

"It's not a who, it's a what. A bite. A bribe."

"What a shame. I thought it was a girl, some gorgeous brunette who's a double or triple agent—you know, the usual thing."

Smedler came out of his office to pick up his mail. He appeared a little too perfectly groomed, as if he'd just been given the full treatment in a beauty salon or a mortician's prep room. "Good morning, Aragon. Great weather, isn't it? On these crisp fall days you can feel the old corpuscles moving right along."

"Yes, sir. It's nice to be back."

Smedler looked surprised. "Have you been away? . . . Has he been away, Miss Nelson?"

"Yes, Mr. Smedler. On a personal mission for Mrs. Decker."

"Ah yes. How'd it go, Aragon?"

"Fine."

"Fine. Now *that's* the kind of answer I appreciate. Pour him a cup of coffee on the house, Miss Nelson."

Smedler returned to his office while Charity put fifteen cents in the coffee machine and extracted a cup of semihot, semicreamed semicoffee.

"Oh, you shouldn't, Miss Nelson," Aragon said. "This is too much, it's beyond the call of duty. You really shouldn't."

"Okay, I won't," she said and drank the coffee herself. "I can type this letter up for you, if you like. How many copies do you need?"

"One."

"One? Nobody ever needs just one. Since this concerns Mrs. Decker, you'll want to give her the ribbon copy and keep a few others for your private files."

"Why will I want to do that?"

"It's standard practice," Charity said. "Don't fight it."

"I have no private files."

"You shouldn't admit anything like that. You'll never get to first base in this business without the basics. Rule one: always have plenty of copies made of everything. The less important the matter is, the more copies you ask for."

"But I only need one. In fact, I don't really need that. Mrs. Decker probably hasn't any files either."

"As a businesswoman I don't know how to deal with people who won't obey the ordinary commonsense business rules."

"I'll tell you how," Aragon said. "Leave us alone. Forget the night letter. It never happened."

"You're getting weird, Aragon. I don't think being a spy agrees with you. Maybe you should try some other line of work, something that keeps you out in the fresh air and sunshine, like a forest ranger. I can picture you ranging the forest in cute little green shorts to match all those leaves ... Don't dash off. I have lots of other suggestions."

"Make twenty copies of each and file them."

The week since he'd first arrived at the house and seen Reed cleaning the pool seemed like a month, and the patio itself was a world or two away from the squalid streets of Rio Seco. Camellias were starting to bloom, pink and perfect in their marble tubs, and the nandina leaves were already tipped with autumn bronze. Reflections of royal blue princess flowers moved back and forth in the sky blue water, rippling the outlines of the ceramic mermaid and softening her tile smirk. She looked real, like a child playing a game of drowning.

Reed was sitting at a glass and aluminum table that was set for two. He wore his working uniform, slacks and a short-sleeved cotton jacket buttoned at the throat. As usual, he wasted no time on amenities. "Sit down. You're early. I can guess why. After a week of the food you get down there, you're half starved."

"I was brought up on that kind of food."

"Yeah? You'll probably have ulcers by the time you're thirty. Do you know how those terribly hot spices came to be used? They were meant to cover the smell and taste of putrescent fish, fowl and animal flesh."

"You're a bundle of information, Reed."

"I know . . . The old girl will be out in a few minutes. She's getting herself all dolled up. What did you tell her? She hasn't fussed like this about her appearance for months. I hope she's not building up to a letdown. Her letdowns are rough on the hired help."

"Are you classed as one of the hired help?"

"Not for long."

"What does that mean?"

"Nothing lasts forever. Right? Sit down, be cool. I made the lunch myself so you wouldn't have to eat the local swill, an austere little casserole of artichoke hearts and eggs in a Ceylonese coconut-milk sauce. I had to break open four coconuts to get the right amount of milk. Violet Smith is having fits about what to do with all the coconut meat. I told her what she could do with all the coconut meat, but she didn't buy the idea. Some people aren't open to suggestion."

"I can see why."

Reed laughed, a bubbly mischievous sound that might have come from the mermaid at the bottom of the pool. "Violet Smith and I are on different wavelengths. To be frank, she doesn't fit into the household. I want Gilly to fire her."

"Gilly?"

"Everybody calls her by her first name—behind her back, anyway. You can't behave the way she behaves and expect to be treated like Queen Elizabeth. Queen Elizabeth doesn't get looped and loud, or exchange insults and jokes with the staff. I don't intend this as criticism of Gilly—it's just her way of dealing with the tremendous emotional strain of Decker's illness."

Feathery scraps of pampas grass drifted across the flagstones and caught in the spikes of the firethorn bushes. The berries were ripe and ready for the winter birds.

Aragon said, "What brought you here in the first place, Reed?"

"I worked in the private hospital where Decker was a patient after his stroke. He took a fancy to me."

"And Mrs. Decker?"

"She also took a fancy to me. Women do. Strange, isn't it, since the fancy can hardly be called mutual. Gilly's a nice old girl, if you like nice and old. And if you like girls."

"You reassure me."

"How come?"

"I've had the notion of something going on between you and Mrs. Decker, that you might even be thinking of marriage after Decker dies and providing B. J. doesn't turn up."

"Oh, come now. Why would I want to get married?"

"To enjoy an early retirement."

"I don't believe in early retirements or marriage. That puts two holes in your theory, enough to kill it, right?"

Aragon brushed some scraps of pampas grass off the table-cloth. They shone in the sun like golden feathers. He said, "I'm beginning to doubt very seriously that B. J. will turn up, either because he can't or because he doesn't want to. As for Decker, I gather he's not going to survive."

"None of us is going to survive, amigo. Decker's number is coming up sooner than most, is all."

"What do you expect will be the actual cause of death?"

"Kidney failure, cerebral hemorrhage, heart congestion, who knows? He's in bad shape in every department. He has only one thing going for him. Gilly. She works her tail off to keep him alive. She won't give up and she won't let him give up. He doesn't really want to live. She's *making* him do it."

"Why?"

"She's a very loyal woman. Stubborn, too. She thinks fate handed Decker a bum deal and she's fighting back. She's a great believer in fair play, justice, all that kind of crap." Reed got up, straightening the jacket of his uniform as if he were going on duty. "I'd better check the casserole. What did you tell Gilly on the phone?"

"That B. J. was released from jail three years ago by a magistrate named Guadalupe Hernandez."

130

"So at least he didn't leave feet first."

"Not according to the records anyway. Hernandez wouldn't give Miss Eckert of the consulate any details, so she suggests trying a little bribery. Or a lot. No sum was specified, but a great many officials lead high lives on low wages, so somebody must be paying."

"And now it's Gilly's turn."

"If she's willing."

"She'll be willing, bet on it. I told you she has this thing about justice and fair play. Well, all her money—except what she gets from Decker—was B. J.'s to begin with. She'll spend every cent of it on him if she has to, the way she spends every ounce of her energy and will on Decker. Probably with the same result. Zero."

The artichoke hearts and eggs lay untouched on Gilly's plate. "How much?"

"I don't know," Aragon said. "I've never bribed a judge."

"You claim a lot of them live high. How high? Like this, for instance—this house, the servants?"

"I think so."

"Offer him a thousand to start. Be prepared to raise the price as much as you have to."

"You assume I'm going back."

"Of course you're going back. Don't you want to?"

"No."

"You're quitting," she said. "Just when the case is beginning to open up, you're quitting."

"No, I'm not. You asked if I wanted to go back and I said no. I have the feeling someone is following me around down there, watching every move I make."

"You're getting paranoid."

"If you prefer to use that word, fine. I'm a paranoid with someone following me around, watching every—"

"You must admit it doesn't sound reasonable, Aragon. I expect a lawyer, even a novice like you, to have a certain objectivity. Someone who's behind you and headed in the same direction as you are isn't necessarily following you. Now, are you going back or aren't you?"

"I am."

"Right away. This afternoon or tonight."

He shook his head. "Sorry. I need a day off to catch up on my mail, my laundry, some—"

"Laundry, mail, all that can wait. You're not helpless. Can't you rinse out your own socks?"

"Yes, dammit, I can rinse out my own socks."

"Then do it. And please try to work up a little enthusiasm for your job."

"I'm trying," he said grimly.

"As for the business about someone tailing you, it's probably a mistake. He may think you're someone else."

"I'm beginning to think the same thing."

"In any case, the solution is very simple. Next time it happens, all you have to do is turn around and confront him—or her—and identify yourself. That ought to solve the problem."

"Or create new ones."

"Please try to take a more positive attitude. I'm trying. I'm trying very, very hard to keep my—well, we won't go into that. You'll need extra money."

"Not yet. Wait until I talk to Hernandez."

"All right." She glanced down at her plate. "What's this crud taste like?"

"I can't describe the taste exactly, but it feels kind of slippery."

"Slippery. Christ." She got up and dumped the contents of her plate in one of the marble tubs containing a camellia bush. The leaves covered the evidence. A dog or cat might smell it out or a bird discover it while searching for insects, but Reed would never see it.

When she returned to the table with the empty plate she looked suddenly old and sick, as if the dumping of the food had been a symbolic gesture, a rejection of life itself.

"You shouldn't go without lunch," Aragon said. "Let me take you out for a burger, guaranteed not slippery."

"That's nice of you, Aragon. I really appreciate it, I'd love a burger and fries, a whole bunch of nice greasy fries. But I can't leave Marco. He's not used to the new nurse yet. I can tell by his pulse that she makes him nervous. It's too bad. Mrs. Morrison has excellent references and Marco has to get used to someone else besides me and Reed. Reed could quit any time. He has no contract, and I have no guarantee that I'll last longer than my husband. It's likely but not certain. I must prepare for every contingency. I promised him he'd never be left alone."

Mrs. Morrison's voice was as crisp and starched as the small pleated white cap which sat on top of her head like a crown. No matter how vigorously she moved her head, the crown remained firmly attached as though she'd been born wearing it and entitled to all the privileges it bestowed.

"I have studied your charts with some care, Mr. Decker," she said regally, "and I have reached the conclusion that the amount of brain damage you have sustained will not prevent us from communicating with each other, at least on an elementary level. Such communication can be arranged in a fairly simple manner. Have you ever played twenty questions? Of course you have. Very well. I will ask you only questions which can be answered by yes or no. You will then raise one finger of your right hand for yes, and two for no. Or if you prefer, blink your right eyelid instead, once for yes, twice for no. Think you can do that?"

He didn't move. He had so much to say that the sheer bulk of it overwhelmed him. His fingers were icicles inside their warm blanket of flesh, and his eyelid felt as though someone had sewn it shut.

"Come, come, you're not going to be uncooperative just because we're strangers, are you? I am your *nurse.* You should trust me to practically the same degree that you trust your doctor or your wife. I am with you, Mr. Decker, *with* you. Let's try a few basic questions for practice. Wait now, did I say one finger or one blink for yes, and two for no, or was it two fingers or two blinks for yes, and one for no? We'd better start over. I think we'll say two fingers or two blinks for yes, and one finger or one blink for no. Ready to begin?"

He opened his right eye and gave her a look of such terrible loathing that even Mrs. Morrison, who was not noted for sensitivity, felt a certain coolness in the air.

"We must *communicate,* Mr. Decker. I'm not a mind reader and you're not a vegetable, appearances to the contrary. Let's make that a test question: Are you a vegetable?"

He wasn't.

"There, that's better, you are not a vegetable. Is your name Marco Decker? No? Are you being deliberately perverse or are you just stupid? This is a serious matter. Is the sun shining? Yes, it *is*, so I want two, *two* for yes. Do you understand me? Another yes, two fingers or two blinks."

All of his powers of concentration and will were gathered now to move his hand.

"Why, you old goat, I do believe that's an obscene gesture."

He blinked twice.

Seventeen

Aragon had been half hoping he wouldn't be able to find it, but he could hardly have missed. It was the only house on Camino de la Cima, an oiled dirt road southeast of the city. The long winding driveway that led up to it was lined with silver-leaved eucalyptus trees that tossed and trembled at the slightest hint of wind.

The whole hillside was enclosed by hurricane fencing with half a dozen rows of barbed wire along the top. At the entrance the double iron-grilled gates were open, and so was the door of the gatehouse itself. The small building had been constructed like a miniature mission with sand-colored adobe walls and red tile roof. It reminded Aragon of the abandoned church in Bahía de Ballenas where the padre lived, but there was a couple of hundred years' difference in age. Another and more important difference quickly became apparent. Instead of a kindly old padre coming to the door, there were two young men wearing uniforms and holsters. One of them also carried a rifle.

They watched with polite interest as Aragon parked his car and approached the gatehouse. Then the man with the rifle nodded and his companion went over to the car. He opened the right front door and looked through the glove compartment and under the seat. Then he took out the ignition keys, unlocked the trunk and searched it. He closed it again and replaced the ignition keys. Hernandez was taking good care of his past *mordidas*.

Aragon said, "Is this the residence of Magistrate Guadalupe Hernandez?"

The man with the rifle did the talking, in a professional monotone. "You have business with the magistrate?"

"Yes. My name is Aragon."

"It is Saturday afternoon, surely not your ordinary business hours, Mr. Aragon."

"This was the only time I could get here. I just arrived from Los Angeles and I was hoping Mr. Hernandez would give me an appointment this afternoon."

"The matter you wish to see him about must be of grave importance."

"No. I simply thought if I could contact him now, I'd be able to go back home tomorrow."

"You don't like our city?"

"It's fine."

"Very fine, I think."

"Yes."

"Finer than Los Angeles?"

"I'll have to consider that for a while."

"Take your time." He dropped his rifle against the gatehouse door. Then he leaned against the wall with his arms crossed on his chest. "I am in no hurry. Salazar, my assistant, is in no hurry either. Are you, Salazar?"

"No, sir," the younger man said. "I am on duty."

"Where would you go if you weren't on duty?"

"To the jai alai games."

"I prefer the bullfights. You don't have bullfights in Los Angeles, Mr. Aragon?"

"No."

"Jai alai. Do you have jai alai?"

"Not to my knowledge."

"What do you do for amusement?"

"Punch out old ladies, kick dogs, stuff like that."

"Ah, most uncivilized."

"Yes."

136

"So you must come here for amusement . . . He won't find the magistrate very amusing today, will he, Salazar?"

"No, sir."

"Certainly I've heard no one laughing."

"Neither have I, sir."

"Perhaps you'd better drive our American visitor up to the house to discover why no one is laughing."

"I'm not sure that would be wise, sir."

"You never do foolish things, Salazar? Then you must start by taking Mr. Aragon up to see Magistrate Hernandez."

"Yes, sir."

The blacktop road that led to the house was about half a mile long. Salazar drove it as though he were practicing for the Indianapolis 500 in low gear. He stopped at the entrance to a carport on the east side of the house. There was space for four cars but only one was in it at the moment, a late-model jeep station wagon.

"Thank you, Salazar," Aragon said. "That was a very interesting ride."

"I am a fine driver, do you think?"

"You are a very fine driver." *Like Rio Seco is a very fine city and your boss is a very fine man.*

Salazar took the keys out of the ignition and handed them to Aragon with a solemn nod of the head. "I have only driven twice before. I guess it is a natural talent."

The main house was a combination of mission and ranch style. Under the wide beamed overhang of the tile roof, about an acre of patio circled the house. It was furnished with dark heavy wooden benches and decorated with glazed clay pots painted in such vivid colors that the plants they contained looked drab by contrast and secondary in importance. Many of the plants were dead or dying, as if the effort of competing with the pots had been too much of a strain.

Under the arch of the main entrance, two Cadillac limousines and a Jensen Interceptor were parked with a chauffeur behind the wheel of each. The three chauffeurs and Salazar were the only people in sight, and the only sound was Salazar's voice: "Someday when I attain a position of importance, I will buy a big car like one of those. Meanwhile I will practice by going to the cinema and watching carefully how they are driven. The important thing is aim."

"Aim?"

"Like a rifle. You aim it just so and it shoots in that direction just so."

Aragon hoped he wouldn't be in the vicinity when Salazar bought his big car and aimed it just so.

An older man came out of one of the side doors. Like Salazar and the gatekeeper, he was in uniform. Either the uniform had been too small to begin with or he'd grown fat in the wearing of it. He was stuffed into it like a sausage balancing on two toothpick legs.

He said to Salazar, "Who is this person?"

"An American who flew in from Los Angeles this afternoon. His name is Aragon."

"Does he speak Spanish?"

"Yes, Superintendent. Very well."

"What does he want?"

"To see Magistrate Hernandez."

"I'm sorry I barged in like this," Aragon said. "If Mr. Hernandez is in the middle of an emergency, I can wait for a later appointment."

The superintendent gazed at him pensively. "Oh no. The emergency has passed."

"Is something the matter around here?"

"Why do you think something is the matter?"

"The security precautions seem excessive."

"Excessive for what?"

"The house of an ordinary magistrate."

"Magistrates have great power in this part of the world. Where there is great power, there are many enemies."

"I assure you I'm not one of them."

"I thought not," the superintendent said. "Enemies don't usually appear at the front gate and give their names. Unless, of course, they're subtle. Which you are not. I consider myself an excellent judge of character and you appear to me a heavy young man—heavy-handed, heavy-footed, heavy-minded. Is this correct?"

"It may be a trifle too flattering."

"Your tone indicates that I hit a nerve. Which nerve?"

"I ran the mile in four ten in college."

"That's good?"

"Yes."

"Very well, we'll take out the heavy-footed. The rest stays. Come inside."

He led the way through a long narrow room that looked like a combination of art gallery, church and library. The books were leatherbound copies of English classics translated into Spanish. The pictures, in ornate gilt frames, were of a religious nature— madonnas, crucifixions, resurrections—except for one large oil painting of a man wearing a magnificent scarlet uniform with gold epaulettes and silver scabbard and sword. A dozen or more candles burned in silver candelabra below the painting and on the altar at the far end of the room.

The superintendent surveyed the room proudly as if it were his own and the man in the scarlet uniform were an earlier self, or at least a relative. "The *galleria* is most impressive, don't you agree, Mr. Aragon?"

"Yes." *I hope this agreeing business starts getting easier. I may have to do a hell of a lot more of it.* "Most impressive."

"But I detect a certain hesitancy in your manner. You're not a religious man, perhaps?"

"Perhaps not."

"Religion can be a great solace for people in trouble."

"Are you implying that I'm in some kind of trouble, Superintendent?"

"What kind of trouble could you be in when you only arrived in Rio Seco this afternoon? You've hardly had time to go out looking for it. Perhaps I can help. Come, I'll show you the magistrate's office."

Beyond the altar was a massive, elaborately carved oak door with iron hinges which creaked a warning when the superintendent pushed the door open.

The room inside was in sharp contrast to the *galleria.* Except for a picture window which offered a view of the main entrance to the house, this was strictly an office, with fluorescent lighting, a mahogany desk with a leather swivel chair, and floor-to-ceiling shelves and files. Nearly every drawer in the desk and the files was open and spilling paper, folders, cards, manila envelopes, letters. A painting hiding a small safe had been pushed aside, but the door of the safe remained closed. In one corner of the room was a small table with two wineglasses and a bottle of Beaujolais on it. The bottle was still full, but it had been uncorked. The cork was lying on the tray with the forced-air opener still stuck in it like a hypodermic needle.

A middle-aged man sitting behind the desk rose when the superintendent and Aragon entered and immediately took Aragon's picture with a Polaroid camera. The pictures he'd already taken were scattered on the desk in front of him. They seemed to be mainly various angles of the disarray in the room.

The superintendent said, "I assume you don't mind having your picture taken."

"That depends on what you're going to do with it."

"I may keep it in my wallet. Then again, I may not. Let's see how it turned out . . . Not bad. Certain physiological characteristics are obscured, others are emphasized. It all balances out, wouldn't you say?"

The superintendent held up the picture and Aragon glanced at it. He hardly recognized himself. The young man in the picture looked confident, almost cocky. He didn't feel either.

"You may have deduced, Mr. Aragon, that someone paid a call on Magistrate Hernandez while he was working. He liked to catch up on his work at night whenever possible so he could spend more of the daylight hours with his children . . . Obviously the call wasn't a friendly one, or at least it didn't end up that way. Kindly remove your spectacles. I believe Ganso here would like another shot."

"Do I have a choice?"

"Of course not."

He removed his spectacles. The second picture showed a little more of the truth. He looked scared. "I hope you don't think I had anything to do with all this. I told you, I just arrived in town."

"But you have been here before in our city?"

"Yes."

"When?"

"I—well, at the beginning of the week. I left Thursday afternoon."

"This is only Saturday afternoon. What made you leave and come back so soon?"

"I received word at my office that Magistrate Hernandez might have news of someone I've been searching for on behalf of a client. I'm a lawyer."

"So? The last man I arrested was a lawyer. His interpretation of the law didn't quite coincide with mine." The superintendent went and stood by the window with the view of the front entrance. "Presumably your client has a name."

"That's privileged information."

"In your country, yes. In mine, no. It's one of the basic differences in our legal systems. Now, the name of your client, please."

"Gilda Grace Decker."

"And she hired you to find someone who also has a name."

"Byron James Lockwood, her former husband."

"How does Magistrate Hernandez fit into all this?"

"Lockwood was serving time in the Quarry for a real estate swindle and Hernandez was responsible for his release three years ago. No one has seen Lockwood since."

"Perhaps," the superintendent said dryly, "Mr. Lockwood doesn't wish to be seen."

"It's possible."

"It is, then, possible that he took steps to make sure he is not seen?"

"What kind of steps?"

"He may have come here to the house, for instance, to destroy some records pertaining to him. That would have been stupid enough, he being an ex-convict and the magistrate an important person. But what followed was surely the ultimate in stupidity . . . Step over here for a minute. I want you to see something."

Aragon went to the window. Some people were coming out of the front door, three men, a stout woman, heavily veiled, leaning on the arm of a fourth man, and half a dozen children ranging in age from five to midteens. The woman and the man escorting her got into the first limousine, and the children into the second. The rest of the group entered the Jensen and all the cars began moving slowly down the driveway.

"See those people," the superintendent said. "Where do you think they are going?"

"I don't know."

"How are they dressed?"

"In black."

"Like mourners, would you say?"

"Yes."

"Where would they be going, dressed like mourners?"

"To a funeral," Aragon said.

Eighteen

For the next three hours Aragon answered questions, many of them repetitious: What was he doing in Rio Seco? What was he actually doing? What was he *really* actually doing? Who was Lockwood? Had he ever met him? What kind of man was he?

"It's unlikely he could have committed any crime of violence," Aragon said. "He was, by all accounts, a very gentle person."

"A lot of gentle persons go into the Quarry and come out not so gentle. You speak of yesterday, I must think of now and tomorrow. Lockwood could be a changed man. You agree?"

"Yes." *I agree again. This time it's real.*

"As you can see"— the superintendent pointed to the table with the opened bottle of wine and the two glasses— "Hernandez was preparing to offer his visitor a drink. Which indicates that either he was a friend or he had come on a friendly mission such as bringing Hernandez something, a gift, say."

"Say a *mordida.*"

"All right, a *mordida.* I don't like the word but it is a fact of life so we'll use it. Certainly we can assume that Hernandez was expecting someone, if not this particular person, because he left the gate open and no one is on duty in the gatehouse at night except on special occasions. So the caller arrived. Let's call him Lockwood."

"Let's not."

"Very well—Mr. Mordida, then. How's that?"

"Better."

"Mr. Mordida drove up to the house and Hernandez let him in. It was obviously an informal visit. Hernandez was wearing a paisley print robe over white silk pajamas. He brought Mr. Mordida here into the office and opened a bottle of wine. Up to this point the meeting was amicable. What happened to change it, I don't know. The children and servants occupy another wing of the house and most of them were sleeping. Mrs. Hernandez heard nothing, no car driving up, no sounds of quarreling or of the office being ransacked. This isn't surprising, since the adobe walls are a foot thick and she was in the bedroom watching television. Shortly after ten o'clock she came to say good night to her husband and found him dead and the room looking like this. She telephoned the doctor, who in turn called me. I came right out with Ganso, my photographer, and several other men. I've been on duty ever since, both here and at the hospital where Hernandez's body was taken to determine the cause of death. There were no marks on him, he gave every evidence of having died naturally of a heart attack or a stroke. Except for the condition of the room, we might have left it at that. Would you like to see some of the pictures Ganso took of the body?"

"Not particularly."

"Ganso likes to take pictures of everything. No one ever looks at them, which is a shame because the film is expensive. Are you sure you—?"

"I'm sure."

"Very well, I'll proceed. When Hernandez's robe was removed at the hospital I noticed a very small spot of blood on the back of his pajama top. It seemed a peculiar place for a bloodstain. If it had been on the front it could have passed as the result of a shaving nick or even a dribble of red wine which, as you can see, Hernandez fancied. After I drew the doctor's attention to the spot he examined Hernandez's back very carefully and found, under the left shoulder blade, a puncture wound made by an extremely thin sharp instrument, something in the nature of an icepick. But I don't believe it was an icepick. You see the forced-air opener still in the cork of the wine bottle over there? I think before it was inserted in the cork, it was inserted in Hernandez. The wound was so small that the skin closed over it almost immediately and all the bleeding, except for that one drop, took place internally. Death occurred fairly quickly, since the weapon penetrated the heart and the pressure of blood in the pericardial sac caused the heart to stop beating. I'm not a medical expert, I'm merely repeating roughly what the doctor told me. Whoever struck the blow was either very lucky or very skillful."

"Lockwood was neither," Aragon said. "All his luck was bad and his only skill seems to have been attracting women."

"That sounds to me like good luck."

"Not for him."

"I could use such luck, call it good or bad." The superintendent stared down at his belly as if he were wondering how it got there. "This Lockwood, he was probably thin?"

"No. In the only pictures I saw of him he was quite fat."

"Tall?"

"No."

"But very handsome?"

"No."

"That's most encouraging, a small fat homely man attracting many women. Yes, I like that very much, it tempts me to view you in a much friendlier light. But such a thing would be unprofessional. I am always professional."

"I can see you are."

"It shows, then?"

"It shows."

The superintendent sat down in the swivel chair behind the desk and Ganso immediately took a picture of him. There was complete silence while the film was developing. The finished product showed a small homely fat man.

The superintendent gazed at it soberly. "I must keep reminding myself of Lockwood and all those women. Were they nice sensible women, the kind a man would choose to marry and to bear his children?"

"I only know one of them. She's—" He wasn't sure that "nice" and "sensible" were the right words to describe Gilly. "She's very interesting."

"Why has she not formed an attachment to some other man?"

"She did. Or at any rate she married him."

"How is it, then, that she wants you to find Lockwood?"

"Her present husband is dying. I think she is afraid of being left alone."

"How old is she?"

"About fifty."

"I am not interested in any woman beyond childbearing age."

"Naturally not." *Poor Gilly will be heartbroken.* "One of the other women is still young, only twenty-three."

"That is much better. And she likes fat homely men?"

"Her personal preferences don't matter. She's a hustler here in Rio Seco. You might know her. In a professional way, of course —your profession, not hers."

"We have a great many hustlers in Rio Seco. Most of their customers are American tourists who drive down for the races or the bullfights, Navy men who drive by the busload from San Diego and Marines from Camp Pendleton."

"Her name is Tula Lopez."

The superintendent shook his head. "The hustlers don't come up to me on the street and introduce themselves. If I were a private citizen and wanted to find a particular young woman, I'd put her name on the grapevine and offer a sum of money for information."

"Or hire a shouter."

"So you have been to the Quarry. Good. That will give you some idea of what happens to people who don't watch their behavior ... Do you know a man named Jenkins?"

"Jenkins is a common name in my country."

"In my country it's most unusual. Thus, when someone named Jenkins performs an unusual act like jumping off our new bridge, it arouses my curiosity and wonderment. Do you have much wonderment, Mr. Aragon?"

"Enough."

"Then let's wonder together about various coincidences. Mr. Jenkins and your friend, Lockwood, were both Americans. Jenkins served time in the Quarry for the same offense that Lockwood did. You tell me that Lockwood was released by Magistrate Hernandez after a payment of some kind. Now I tell you that Jenkins also was released by this same Magistrate Hernandez after paying a fine. What do you make of all this?"

146

"That Hernandez had ways of supplementing his income."

"His income wouldn't have bought the rug on this floor. Our public servants are very poorly paid, that is why they become private bosses. A little *mordida* here, and a little there, keeps them from starving."

"Hernandez was about as far from starving as I am from being named to the Supreme Court."

"*Mordida* is part of your system too, so I hope you didn't come riding across the border on a white horse."

"I don't ride a horse of any color," Aragon said. "Just a ten-speed bicycle."

"I dislike all forms of exercise except that of the imagination. From the neck up I am very athletic. I am like a greyhound chasing a mechanical rabbit at the dog track. Only *I* catch the rabbit . . . You smile, I see, because I don't look like a greyhound. Well, you don't look like a rabbit. But here we both are."

Aragon had already stopped smiling. "I'm not sure what a greyhound would do to a real rabbit if he caught one."

"Probably nothing. The chase is what matters to him. But the rabbit doesn't know that. What matters to him is escape. Sometimes he makes a serious error and runs into a hole which has no exit. That's what you did. You ran right up that driveway and into this house."

"My coming here was a coincidence."

"I can swallow only a certain number of coincidences. Then I start to upchuck. So let's eliminate some of these coincidences, shall we?"

"I don't know how."

"We'll begin once more at the beginning."

The superintendent got up, walked around the room quite rapidly as if his athletic imagination were chasing him, then sat down again in the swivel chair. Aragon stared out the window, but it was dark. All he could see was the reflection of the room itself, the fat man in uniform behind the desk, the middle-aged man with the camera poking around in the clutter of ransacked papers, and the young man standing at the window peering through his horn-rimmed glasses like a rabbit that had entered a hole with no exit.

"No, Mr. Aragon, tell me frankly, what brought you here this afternoon?"

"A telegram from someone at the U.S. consulate who found out that Lockwood had been released from prison by Magistrate Hernandez."

"Did you expect to see the magistrate?"

"Yes."

"And to ask him questions?"

"Yes."

"And to receive answers?"

"Yes."

"*Mordidas,*" the superintendent said, "do not appear in filing cabinets or record books. Or magistrates' answers."

"I thought it was worth a try, since my previous attempts to find Lockwood failed."

"Now this one has also failed. What will be your next step?"

"I think I'll go home."

"But there is still the girl. Aren't you going to look for her?"

"No."

"Why not?"

"I'm afraid to."

"Afraid? You're strong, young—"

"I'm not afraid for myself. I do all right. I don't back into sharp instruments or fall off bridges."

"So . . ." The superintendent leaned his elbows on the desk and the tips of his fingers came together to frame an arch like a bridge. "So you *did* know Jenkins."

"I never said I didn't."

"You implied as much."

"I evaded the question. I wanted to make sure you were an intelligent and reasonable man."

"And now that you've made sure, you will tell me everything?"

"Everything isn't much," Aragon said. "First I got Jenkins' address from his girl friend in the Quarry."

"Her name, please."

"Emilia Ontiveros."

"Why is she in the Quarry?"

"For assault. Assault on Jenkins."

"This Jenkins apparently didn't have a way with women like Lockwood."

"It wouldn't have mattered. Miss Ontiveros is the jealous type. Anyway, Jenkins claimed that he'd lost contact with Lockwood and had no idea where he was. For a sum of money he agreed to find Tula Lopez for me. I think he found her, but he never had a chance to tell me and to collect the rest of his money. I had paid him fifty dollars in advance and promised him two hundred more for Tula Lopez. She'd borne Lockwood a child. I figured there might still be some kind of bond between them and she could possibly put me in touch with him if he's alive, or tell me what happened to him if he's dead."

"Two hundred dollars to find a hustler in these parts, that's real inflation for you. They used to be a dime a dozen, and for fifty cents they'd throw in a free case of V.D. They're somewhat cleaner now. The tourists were complaining. *Turista* in Rio Seco did not always involve the digestive track . . . Tell me more about Jenkins."

"The fifty dollars was found in his pocket when they picked up the pieces. It paid for his funeral. It wasn't much of a funeral —I'm sure Hernandez did better."

Aragon thought of the mourning party leaving the house in the Cadillacs and Jensen, the black-veiled widow with her starched and scrubbed children, the dignified, formally dressed men. They hadn't yet returned. They were probably still at church, praying for Hernandez's soul and paying for the candles with some of his *mordidas.*

"I am still upchucking coincidences," the superintendent said. "A little wine might help settle my stomach. Would you care for some?"

Aragon glanced over at the table with the bottle of wine on it and the impaled cork. "From that bottle?"

"Certainly. Red wine should always be served at room temperature."

"What I meant was, I thought it would be considered evidence."

"I see no harm in drinking a little of the evidence. There'll be enough left." The superintendent poured two glasses of wine, gave one to Aragon and raised the other in a toast. "To crime. Without it we'd both be unemployed. Drink up."

"I prefer not to."

"Squeamish?"

"I was imagining what would happen to me back home if I were found drinking some of the evidence in a murder case."

"A bad thing would happen?"

"Very bad. Maybe terminal."

"Ah well, we're more civilized here. A little evidence is just as good as a lot." He drank both glasses of wine, pronounced it mediocre, wished aloud for some bleu cheese to go with it, poured a third glass and settled back in the swivel chair again. "This client of yours, the lady who is about fifty and likes fat homely men, she must be rich."

"Yes."

"Is she Catholic?"

"No."

"I can be ecumenical when necessary. Is she really very rich, do you suppose?"

"Yes."

"You know, Aragon, I could change my mind about wanting a family. After all, it might be a mistake for a man my age to start a family if he has the opportunity to marry a mature rich woman. This line of thought appeals to me suddenly. What do you think?"

"I think no."

"Why no?"

"For starters, Mrs. Decker is already married, she doesn't speak Spanish, she has strong opinions and states them bluntly, and she's pretty tight with a buck."

"But as her husband I would control her money."

"No."

"I would be boss."

"No."

"Ah well, there are other fish in the sea," the superintendent said.

He postponed his report to Gilly until after he'd had dinner and some tequila in the form of three margaritas. He decided to make the call as brief as possible in the hope of avoiding any histrionics, recriminations, hindsights or whatever she was offering, so after a brief exchange of amenities he said. "There's an item in tonight's newspaper. You'd better hear it."

150

"No. Wait. Maybe I'd rather not. Your voice sounds funny."

"I've been talking for four hours."

"What about? No, don't tell me. There's something wrong, of course. There always is when the phone rings late at night like this and it's you on the line."

He didn't say anything."

"Aragon? Operator, I think I've been cut off. Aragon, are you there? What are you doing?"

"Waiting for you to shut up."

"That's rude," Gilly said. "That's damn bloody rude."

"I know."

"Aren't you going to apologize?"

"Not unless I have to."

"I don't believe in *forced* apologies. What good are *forced* apologies?"

"Beats me."

"You've been drinking again. It's obvious from your impertinence."

"I'm having my third margarita."

"You'll turn into a lush if you keep this up. Does alcoholism run in your family?"

"Shucks, no. There was just Mom and Dad, and my grandparents on both sides, and my uncles Manuel and Reginato, and my Aunt Maya—she could really belt the booze—"

"Oh, shut up."

"I will if you will."

She did, for a minute. "Is it—do you have bad news?"

"It was bad for Hernandez and not so good for me. Are you ready to listen now?"

"Yes."

"Okay. 'Magistrate Guadalupe Hernandez, well-known in Rio Seco legal circles, died last night of a stab wound inflicted during an attempted burglary of his foothill residence. Magistrate Hernandez maintained an office in his home and it was in this room that the crime occurred. It is not known what was stolen from the ransacked office. No suspects have been arrested, but Superintendent Playa of the Police Department is following several important leads. The magistrate's survivors include his wife, Carmela Maria

Espinosa, six children, three brothers and a sister. Requiem high mass will be recited Sunday evening at Her Lady of Sorrows Church.' That's it, Mrs. Decker."

"Does this mean you never even talked to him?"

"It means," Aragon said, "that someone reached him before I did. Any man who lives the way he lived makes enemies. Maybe one of them tried to get his *mordida* back."

" 'Ransacked office.' What was ransacked?"

"Desk drawers, filing cabinets, everything. Even if Hernandez were alive to supervise the work, it would take a week to put things together again. As matters stand now, it will probably never be known for sure if any particular file is missing, such as one about B. J. and the circumstances of his release and his present whereabouts."

"How do you know such a file ever existed?"

"I don't. It probably didn't, and even more probably doesn't."

"So we've come to another dead end."

"Dying, anyway."

"How I hate those words, 'dead,' 'dying.' But God knows I should be used to them by now."

"Please," Aragon said, "don't go into a poor-little-me routine. I've been on the grill a long time tonight and I still have some sore spots. Which is better than being in jail."

"Did they put you in jail?"

"Almost."

"What crime did you commit?"

"I didn't commit anything. You don't have to commit anything to land in jail here. You just have to look as though you did or might or could."

"I never thought you looked especially criminal." Gilly said. "Perhaps a little on the sly side at times. You know, cunning, crafty. Maybe it's your glasses. Do you have to wear them?"

"No, I wear them for fun."

"You don't have to sound so mad. It was a perfectly simple question. Everyone seems awfully touchy tonight. Reed got mad at me because I refused to fire Marco's new nurse. He's jealous. She's a good nurse and I enjoy talking to her. He won't admit that I have to see other people for a change instead of spending all my time listening to him yak about food and Violet Smith about religion. Poor Reed. I think he'd like to marry me, but someone got his bootees mixed up in the nursery."

"Marry you?"

"Not me as in me, me as in money."

"How do you feel about it?"

"He's a boy. Boys are for girls. Or in Reed's case, for other boys. If he should ever become insistent, I'll give him a nice bonus and tell him to get lost. He'll be leaving eventually, anyway, when Marco—" The sentence dangled unfinished like a half-knotted noose. "All right, your job's over, Aragon. You might as well come home."

"My other trip home lasted less than forty-eight hours."

"This one will be permanent. I'm tired, you're tired."

"I have to stay here awhile."

"You're to come back now," she said sharply. "We'll settle the account. It's probably cost me a bundle already, bribing half the people in Baja and paying for all the margaritas you've been swilling."

"Margaritas don't swill easy. I charge extra."

"By the way, I intend to go over your expense account line by line."

"Do that. I'll submit it to you when I return."

"Which will be tomorrow."

"No."

"You're not hearing me, Aragon. I said—"

"I heard you and I said no. I'm going to stay here and look for the girl."

"Wait. Listen to me—"

"Good night, Gilly."

He put down the phone and ordered another margarita to see if it could be swilled. It couldn't. He used it to clean his teeth—it had a very stimulating effect on the gums—and went to bed.

Nineteen

It was Sunday.

The fog of the previous night had been driven back to sea by the sun. The wet leaves of the camellias were dark-green mirrors, and the cypress trees were covered with drops of water that caught the sun and looked like tiny glass Christmas balls.

"A beautiful day," Gilly told Marco when she brought his breakfast. "It's so clear, the mountains look as though you could reach out and touch them. When Mrs. Morrison gets here she'll wheel you around to the front of the house so you can see them for yourself . . . I know you don't like her, but you will. And Reed can't work every day. He went to see his mother at a rest home in Oxnard, she's a little balmy. That's his story, anyway. Actually, I'm not even sure he has a mother. But he must have had at one time or another, so what does it matter?"

He stared, one-eyed, at the ceiling.

"The sky? There's not a cloud in sight and it's very blue, like cornflowers. Remember the cornflowers I wore at our wedding? I wanted to keep them but you said not to bother, there'd be a thousand others. But I've never seen any since that were quite that blue."

He was sorry.

"Oh well, they'd be faded by this time, anyway. It's not important. I must keep reminding myself to separate what's important from what isn't." She pulled open the drapes. Beyond the tips of his pygmy forest of plants, the sea shimmered like molten silver. "The kelp beds look purple . . . I wonder why they call that war decoration the Purple Heart. Do you know?"

He didn't know. He'd almost forgotten there was such a thing. What else had he forgotten? A minute here, a week there, or great whole chunks of time? Things were moving inside his head, in directions he could no longer control. Sometimes they met and merged, or they broke off and parts disappeared.

Years flowed in and flowed out of his mind like tides, leaving pools of memories full of small living things. Sometimes the tides stopped, the pools dried up and nothing lived in them any longer. A strange man came and helped him move his bowels. A strange woman sat beside him, claiming to be his wife. Another strange woman had been sent by the Lord to save him, but he didn't know from what. Strangers walked in and out while Gilly and Violet Smith and Reed hid behind clouds or in forests under snow, disappeared around corners and below horizons.

But today was very clear. It was today. The woman was Gilly, his wife. Soldiers got Purple Hearts for being wounded in action. Purpleheart was also a timber from South America named for its color. Masses of kelp looked purple from a distance; close up they were copper-colored and the leaves felt slimy when you swam over them. The woman with the morning newspaper and the glass of orange juice with the plastic tube in it was his wife, Gilly. She was a little balmy, like Reed's mother.

She cranked up his bed and put the plastic tube in his mouth. "Drink up."

He drank. He would have liked to tell her about the timber purpleheart, but she probably wouldn't consider it important. Now that she was dividing things up into important and nonimportant, he wondered where he belonged. Maybe in the middle, leaning toward the non.

"That's a good boy," she said when he finished the orange juice. "Are you hungry this morning?"

No. But he let the egg slither down his throat.

"Violet Smith made you some of her special Sunday toast."

The toast was cut into cubes, soaked in warm milk and sprinkled with cinnamon and sugar and wheat germ. She spooned it into his mouth, giving him several minutes to swallow each spoonful. During these intervals she read aloud items from the newspaper.

Threat of a local bus strike was now believed ended. A government building on Downing Street had been bombed by the IRA. Dow-Jones went up twenty-four points during the past week. Heavy rains in Northern California were expected to hit the lower part of the state late tomorrow or Tuesday. Nine students were shot a few miles from Buenos Aires. A Los Angeles woman was found guilty of embezzling thirty thousand dollars from Crocker National Bank. The Coast Guard rescued a young couple becalmed five miles from shore in a small sailboat.

"I don't see anything in the paper about the magistrate who was murdered in Rio Seco. Aragon told me about it last night on the phone. Hernandez I believe his name was. It's a funny coincidence, isn't it, that he was the magistrate who took a bribe to release B. J. from jail. What a vicious man he must have been, allowing people to rot in jail until they got enough money to buy their way out. He deserved to be murdered, don't you think so, dear?"

He went on swallowing Violet Smith's special Sunday toast. It tasted like Monday morning.

Violet Smith came for the tray. She was dressed for church in a brown suit with an elaborate feathered hat given to her by a former employer. She talked across and around Marco almost as if he'd died during the night and no one had bothered to move the body.

"Did he like the toast, Mrs. Decker?"

"He didn't complain," Gilly said dryly.

"What do you think of my hat, is it too dressy?"

"No."

"Since I'm not allowed to wear jewelry any more, I thought a few feathers would liven things up . . . Is he through?"

"Yes."

"Poor soul, I hope he can't taste too good. That wheat-germ

stuff is nauseous. Reed bought it for his virility last week." Violet Smith picked up the tray. "I wonder if I could speak to you in private for a minute. I don't want him to hear. He has enough trouble already."

"I've told you before, Mr. Decker doesn't like to be talked about as if he's not here."

"Well, he's not really *here,* is he?"

"He's here, dammit."

He was there. It was today. The bickering women were Violet Smith and his wife, Gilly. He wished they'd go away and come in again as two strangers. Strangers were easier to bear.

They talked in the hall, with Marco's door closed. Rays of the sun slanted through the skylight, and the feathers in Violet Smith's hat iridesced and looked alive.

"I've been turning this over and over in my mind," she said, "until I'm on the verge of a sinking spell. I'm not sure what's right and what's not. There's such a thing as minding your own business and then there's such a thing as avoiding your responsibility."

"Get to the point."

"You told me I was never to talk in church about any of the things that happen here at the house—Mrs. Lockwood and all that hanky-panky—and I never did. I never so much as mentioned Mr. Lockwood. *She* did."

"Who?"

"Ethel Lockwood, his first wife. She brought up the subject at the last meeting. I tried to stop her." She couldn't recall saying from the back of the room, *Speak up, I can't hear you.* And if such a memory had struggled its way into her conscious mind, she would have disowned it. "Mrs. Lockwood was determined to continue."

"I can't prevent her from talking," Gilly said. "About Mr. Lockwood or anything else."

"But she's saying bad things."

"How bad?"

Violet Smith's wooden face was splintered by uncertainty. "We're honor-bound not to tell outsiders what goes on at the meetings and I'm scared. He is listening Up There. You better go and see Mrs. Lockwood for yourself."

"I don't want to. I haven't seen her in years."

157

"You better, anyway. She's a little odd, which aren't we all, but she knows something you don't and you ought to."

"Concerning B. J.?"

"Yes."

"Is it important?"

"I wouldn't be standing here talking like this with Him listening Up There if it wasn't important." Violet Smith's feathers were quivering. "Do you want me to tell you her address?"

"I know her address," Gilly said. "Ethel and I are old friends."

Twenty

She remembered the last time she'd seen the house.

B. J. was waiting to let her in. His face was flushed with excitement and anticipation.

"We'll have the whole house to ourselves for a week. Ethel's gone to visit her sister in Tucson and I'm supposed to be staying at the University Club while she's away. Isn't that marvelous?"

It was marvelous.

They used the guest room, which had a king-size bed with a blue silk spread that wrinkled. Afterward B. J., still naked, tried to iron out the wrinkles with his hands. He looked foolish and helpless. She loved him desperately.

"Next time," she said, "we'll take the spread off."

"Next time?" He couldn't cope with this time, let alone think about a next time. He glanced over at the suitcase she'd brought as if he couldn't recall carrying it upstairs for her and putting it on the rack at the foot of the bed. "Maybe you shouldn't actually move in, G. G. It might be better if we met at a motel."

"I want to stay here. I love this room. I love you."

"That damn spread, it'll be the first thing she notices. Why couldn't she have picked some material that doesn't wrinkle?"

"You mustn't be afraid of her."

"She might faint. She faints a lot."

"What if *I* fainted? Right this minute?"

"Oh hell, G. G., you wouldn't. I mean ... would you?"

"I guess not. I'm trying, but I can't seem to get the hang of it."

She sat down on the bed again, deliberately, heavily.

"For God's sake," he said. "Get off there."

"No."

"You don't *realize*—"

"I realize. I just want you to love me so much that you don't care about anything else in the world."

"That's crazy."

"So I'm crazy. Do you love me anyway?"

"Sure I do. But Ethel brought that spread all the way from Hong Kong."

"Maybe if we're lucky she'll take it back to Hong Kong."

He began to laugh in spite of himself at the image of Ethel dragging the spread all the way back to Hong Kong.

Later he was sober again, and scared. Gilly wasn't. "I don't care," she said, "if Ethel walks in right this minute." She didn't. She walked in five days later. She and her sister had an argument and Ethel came home early. She was shocked, disgusted, reproachful. She sobbed, she fainted, she screamed. Then she went back to her sister's in Tucson to think things over.

B. J. thought things over too. "She doesn't really like me, you know. I don't blame her. I'm no prize."

"You are to me," Gilly said.

"You weren't kidding when you said you were crazy. Me a prize. That's a laugh."

"It's true."

"What do you suppose I should do now?"

"Get a divorce and marry me."

"Is this—are you *proposing* to me?"

"Yes."

"Women aren't supposed to do that, G. G. They're supposed to wait to be asked."

"I waited. You never asked."

"How could I? I'm married."

"I'm not. So I'll do the asking. Will you marry me?"

"Well, for Christ's sake—"

"Leave Christ out of it. It's you and me, B. J."

B. J. consulted a lawyer and moved to the University Club. Ethel sent the bedspread to the dry cleaner. Gilly started shopping for a trousseau. If a shadow of remorse appeared now and then, she closed her eyes or turned her back. *It's you and me, B. J.*

From a distance the big white stucco house looked the same. But as she approached, Gilly saw that the paint was peeling off the walls and the window frames. The trees in the courtyard had turned brown from lack of water and were dropping their leaves in the dry birdbath and the empty lily pond. A black cat crouched on top of the wall as if he were waiting for Halloween or for the birdbath to be filled. It watched with green-eyed interest as Gilly walked through the courtyard and pressed the chime of the front door.

This time it was Ethel who let her in.

"I've been expecting you," she said. "Violet Smith called to tell me you were on your way."

"I don't know exactly what I'm doing here."

"You will. Come inside."

"We can talk out here."

"Are you afraid I've arranged some kind of trap for you? How quaint. I assure you I bear no grudges and I have forgiven all my enemies. Come, you'll want to see the changes in the house."

Gilly went inside, wondering about the changes and whether the blue silk bedspread had been one of them. Probably the first.

The living room was lavishly furnished, but it had the pervasive chill of a place that was never used. A layer of dust covered everything, like a family curse, the red velvet chairs and marble-topped tables, the gilt-framed portraits of plump gentle women and stiff-necked men. Silver vases for rosebuds, and crystal bowls made to float camellias, were empty. Spiderwebs hung undisturbed across the chandeliers, and there were cracks in the plaster of the ceiling as though the house had been shaken by a series of explosions.

There were matching cracks in Ethel's face, dividing it into sections like a relief map. She was very thin. Everything about her was thin, her arms and legs, her graying hair, even her skin looked transparent. The blue veins in her temples seemed barely covered.

"It's rude to stare." She spoke just above a whisper, hissing slightly over the *s* sounds. The effect was soft and deadly like

161

escaping gas. "I told you there were changes. I can't afford to keep the place up."

"B. J. left you well provided for."

"He did. But times change—increasing taxes, inflation, some bad investments, a loan to an old friend. No wild extravagances, simply normal living, yet in a few years a house begins to look like this. B. J. would be distressed to see it."

"Don't worry, he won't see it."

"No? You might be wrong."

"What makes you say that?"

"ESP, perhaps. Perhaps something a good deal more practical ... Gracious, I'm forgetting my manners. Please sit down. The wing chairs by the fireplace are very comfortable, but then, you know that, don't you? Now, how shall I address you? I don't believe it would be quite appropriate to call you Gilly or G. G., As B. J. did. B. J. and G. G. How sweet."

"My name is Mrs. Decker. I prefer to stand."

"Very well." She herself sat down in one of the wing chairs and began stroking its red velvet upholstery very gently as though soothing an elderly family pet. "You mustn't think Violet Smith has been indulging in idle gossip. She felt compelled to tell me certain facts."

"Such as?"

"That you were attempting to locate B. J. and the trail ended in the Rio Seco jail, where he is believed to have died."

"And why did Violet Smith feel compelled to tell you all this?"

"Because your facts and mine don't agree. That loan to an old friend I mentioned a few minutes ago, it wasn't actually for an old friend."

"It was for B. J.?"

"Yes."

"When?"

"Three years ago. He didn't die in jail. I paid ten thousand dollars to get him out of there. It wasn't easy to collect that much extra cash. I sold some of my antiques and borrowed the rest from my sister. I know the money arrived safely. He wrote me a thank-you note after his release, just a line or two, without any return address. I didn't keep it. I guess I was piqued because it was so short, so—almost ungracious. I don't think he'd ever accepted money from a woman before and perhaps it hurt his pride." There was a ragged edge of doubt in her voice. "I still have the first letter, though, the one where he asked for the money. That was gracious, oh yes, very gracious indeed. I want you to read it."

"Why?"

"So you won't have to take my word for anything."

"I take it."

"Don't you think it would be better if you took his? Here."

The letter Gilly had received five years before had been written on heavy bond, engraved *Jenlock Haciendas, Bahía de Ballenas, Baja California Sur.* This one was on a kind of onionskin paper Gilly hadn't seen since she was a child. It was postmarked Rio Seco and the return address was the Quarry: LA CANTERA, PENITENCIARIA DEL ESTADO.

Dear Ethel:

I don't know how to start this letter because I shouldn't be writing it not to you of all people. I treated you rotten. You have every right and reason to tear this up before you go any further. But please don't. I haven't anyone else to turn to. I am locked in this terrible place which is so terrible you couldn't bear to come inside the gate. I remember that day we went to the pound to claim Angel, how you cried just seeing the animals locked up. Well now I'm one of them . . .

Gilly said, "Who was Angel?"

"Our Yorkshire terrier."

"I didn't know B. J. ever had a dog." It was such a small thing, completely unimportant, but it bothered her. It made her realize that he'd had a whole life before she even met him, that he'd been married to Ethel twice as long as to her.

I'm in this filthy cage Ethel and I didn't do anything to hurt people. I just thought it was a good idea to bring some prosperity to that God forsaken village I was stuck in. Why am I always being *stuck* in places? It must be lack of character like you told me once. It really hurt me your saying that. I was never sure what character was so how could I get any.

I keep wishing I could start over or at least go back to the point where I began making bad mistakes. You are the only woman I ever truly loved and admired and respected. I could never live up to your standards. None of the other women had class like you Ethel. That's why they appealed to me I guess because they were no better than I was which wasn't much ...

Gilly's hands had begun to tremble. The paper made little rustling sounds like evil whispers. "He was desperate. People tell lies when they're desperate."
"Or truths."
"There's not a word of truth in—"
"Go on reading."

I don't understand how it all happened between Gilly and me. She was a lot of fun and we had some laughs but then suddenly she was expecting me to marry her. She asked me to, I'm not kidding. I was flattered. I had to really talk fast to get you even to *consider* marrying me and here was this other woman anxious to have me. I'm not making excuses Ethel. I just want you to realize that often things just *happen* to people like me. Ordinary people must see things coming and duck maybe, or fight back or run away. But there are some of us who don't see what's coming and we end up in a place like this. I won't try to describe it for you. You wouldn't believe it anyway being you're so clean in mind and body. Do you still take all those showers every day? My God what I'd give for a long hot shower right now. To be clean again what a luxury that would be. Everybody and everything at the Quarry is slimy. It's funny how the people in the U.S. have so many nicknames for prison like it was kind of a joke—pokey, slammer, clink, brig, cooler, tank etc. Here nobody ever calls it anything but the Quarry. It's too serious to have a nickname. I must get out. I *must*.
Ethel you are the only hope I have left. One of the guards told me that my case is finally coming up next month. I can't explain how this crazy system works but it's not the way ours does with a jury, etc. The man who is the magistrate assigned to me will decide my fate. Word from the grapevine is that he charges a fixed price to release Americans $10,000. Guilt and innocence and justice they're only words here. No matter what I did nor didn't do, for $10,000 I can get out of this place.
Please help me. Please for the love of God help me Ethel. I'm going to die here unless you get me out. I am filthy. My clothes, my cot, the food I eat, it's all filthy. My teeth are rotting and my hair is falling out and my eyes are so bad I can hardly see what I'm writing. I've paid a

hundred times for every hurt I've done anyone. I can't take it much longer. I am at your mercy Ethel.

B. J.

Gilly folded the letter and put it back in the envelope very quickly so that Ethel might not notice how badly her hands were trembling. She felt sick, as if someone had struck her a mortal blow in the stomach, and the lump in her throat was so large and heavy that she was afraid her voice couldn't push past it: "Why did you ask me to read this?"

"So you'd understand how useless it is for you to go on searching for B. J. Even if you found him, he wouldn't want to live with you anyway. He turned to *me* in his hour of need, not you. It's all there in the letter. I am the only woman he ever loved and admired and respected."

"Shut up, damn you! Shut your vicious mouth, you—"

"B. J. was right," Ethel said softly. "You have no class."

During the afternoon Gilly cried, sometimes for B. J., sometimes for herself. Mrs. Morrison gave her two pills and Violet Smith brought her the kind of drink Violet Smith had often made for her own consumption before she'd taken the pledge.

When she finally ran out of tears she used eye drops to clear her eyes, and witch hazel pads to reduce the swelling, and make-up to obscure the lines of grief around her mouth. Then she walked across the hall to her husband's room.

She said, without looking at him, "I went to see Ethel Lockwood this morning. She showed me the letter she got from B. J. in prison."

He moved his head. He didn't want to hear about it. Everything was far away and long ago. Who was Ethel?

"The letter had a number of interesting things in it, personal things about me. The consensus of opinion is that I have no class. Imagine that. I always thought I was such a classy dame. Didn't you?"

He knew what was coming.

"Also, I'm dirty. I don't stand around in the shower all day, so I'm dirty."

He could hear the note in her voice that meant she was going to throw a fit and nothing and nobody could stop her. Not even Mrs. Morrison, who thrust her head inside the door and asked if there was anything she could do.

"Yes," Gilly said. "You can drop dead."

"I told you to lie down and rest after taking those pills. I naturally assumed—"

"You can assume right up your ass to your armpits."

"Your knowledge of anatomy is rather meager." Mrs. Morrison turned her attention to the wheelchair. "I'll be out in the hall if you need me, Mr. Decker. Press the buzzer and I'll hear it. I'll probably hear a great many other things as well, but it is my duty to stick with my patient in fair weather *or* foul. Press your buzzer. Have you got that, Mr. Decker? Signify that you understand me by raising two fingers of your right hand for yes. Or did we agree on one finger for yes and two for no? I'm not sure. No matter. Buzz."

"You buzz," Gilly said. "Buzz off."

"I shall be in the hall, Mr. Decker. Listening."

He lay silent and motionless, wishing all the women would go away and never come back, Mrs. Morrison and Violet Smith and Gilly, and now this other one, Ethel. Who was Ethel?

Gilly described her briefly. Ethel was a vicious-tongued, sanctimonious snotty old bitch.

"Where'd she get the right to criticize me? I have as much class as she has. Goddamn it, I'm a classy dame. Are you listening? Do you hear that, you nosy parker out in the hall? I'm a classy dame!"

She began to cry again.

"You know what it said in the letter? It said, 'I don't understand how it all happened between Gilly and me. She was a lot of fun and we had some laughs, but then suddenly she was expecting me to marry her. She asked me to.' That's what it said in the letter, making it sound like I begged, like I was lower than low."

Tears and more tears.

He wished he could offer her some comfort or explanation, anything to stop the deluge that threatened to wash them both out to sea. *We are drowning, Gilly and I, we are drowning together.*

Twenty-one

Aragon spent Sunday driving the rutted roads and walking the dusty streets of Rio Seco. He began near the shoemaker's shop where Jenkins had lived and worked his way past the tinsmiths and weavers and potters and wood-carvers into the red-light district of sleazy bars and sin shows and cubicles where the prostitutes lived and worked and died. He talked to peddlers, cabbies, hookers, *mariachis*. None of them had heard of Tula Lopez.

At eight o'clock he returned to his hotel to have dinner. The clerk on duty at the desk when he stopped to pick up his room key was the same elderly man who'd given him the insecticide on the first night of his stay. He looked nervous. "You like it here at our hotel, sir?"

"It's fine."

"No more mosquitoes?"

"Nothing I can't handle." *I drink beer and the mosquitoes siphon it off before it can damage my liver. It's a pretty fair system.*

"I was telling Superintendent Playa what a quiet and polite young man you were for an American."

"And why did you tell the superintendent that?"

"Because he asked."

"That seems like a good reason."

"I thought so." Some crazy insect was hurling itself at the

light above the desk, and the clerk watched it for a while with a kind of detached interest. "*Why* the superintendent asked, I don't know. But you will certainly find out."

"Certainly?"

"Oh yes. He's waiting for you in the dining room. Since seven o'clock. Already he's eaten one dinner and may have finished a second by this time. Naturally, we cannot present him with a check. It would be unwise. Yet it hardly seems fair that the hotel should pay, since the reason he's here is you. Once in a while a policeman comes to the hotel, but never so important a one and never one with such a huge appetite."

"Put his dinners on my bill."

"What if you are not available later to pay the bill? Possibly you would like to settle your account tonight."

"No, I wouldn't like that."

"What if I insist?"

"I wouldn't like that, either."

"Perhaps you are not so polite an American as I thought," the clerk said and grabbed at the insect that was attacking the light over the desk. He missed. Aragon left the two of them battling it out.

Superintendent Playa, wearing civilian clothes, sat in a corner of the dining room behind a potted palm as though he were in hiding. But there was too much of him to hide, and it seemed inevitable that more of him was on its way. He was eating flan with whipped cream, and drinking something thick and yellowish out of a glass mug.

"Oh, Mr. Aragon. Good evening."

"Good evening, Superintendent."

"I've been waiting for you, passing the time with a bite to eat. Please sit down."

"All right."

"Join me in a *rompope*. It's an eggnog flavored with rum. Quite delicious."

"No thanks."

"Very well, we'll get down to business." The superintendent unbuckled the belt of his trousers, and his stomach ballooned out between him and the table like an air safety bag inflating on impact. "The word is that you've been searching for the girl Tula Lopez all over town."

"Yes."

"You still want to see her?"

"Very much."

"Perhaps I can arrange it. Yes, I think it would be quite possible."

"You know where she is?"

"I know. Come along, we'll pay her a call."

"I haven't had any dinner."

"I ate for both of us to save time."

"That's very good of you."

"You might really believe that, a little later on. If one is going to feel squeamish, it is better to do so on an empty stomach." He rose with some difficulty and pushed his own stomach back into the captivity of its belt. Then he called for his check.

Aragon said, "I told the clerk to add it to my bill."

"Why would you do such a thing? Have you a guilty conscience?"

"No."

"Are you attempting to influence my judgment?"

"No."

"Then why should you pay for my dinner as if I'd been your invited guest?"

"I—"

"Unless, of course, you invited me and the invitation failed to reach me in time. Could that be true?"

"It could."

"Then I accept your hospitality. Many of my invitations arrive late or never. Our local system of communications is poor, though I believe you and I are communicating quite nicely, are we not?"

"I think so."

"Then let us proceed on our way."

The superintendent was driving his personal car, a Toyota not much bigger than he was. He handled it as though it were his alter ego, with courteous attention and respect. Other motorists honked at him from behind, put their heads out windows to curse him as they passed, looked back and shook their fists. The superintendent didn't let it bother him.

"Peasants," he said amicably. "I save my wrath for more significant occasions. Besides, I have a full stomach. There is nothing more soothing than a good meal, isn't that correct?"

"I don't remember. I haven't had one lately."

"Try not to be waspish, Mr. Aragon. I am, after all, doing you a favor. You could have spent a week, even a month, searching for this girl, and I found her for you. You must learn the art of gratitude."

"I don't want to be grateful until I know what I'm being grateful for."

They had reached the bridge. The superintendent was driving very slowly in spite of the pressure of traffic. "Let's see now. It was right about here, from this spot, that your friend Harry Jenkins jumped. No manner of death is pleasant but it seems to me Jenkins picked, or was granted, one of the better ones, leaping out into the air like a bird, then dropping into oblivion. Magistrate Hernandez had no choice, no such beautiful moment of flying. It was quick, though. Others are not so lucky."

She had put up a struggle.

For Tula, there'd been no easy bird flight, no sudden halt of the heart. Deep-purple bruises covered her face and arms and throat. A patch of her hair had been pulled out by the roots and was caught in the splinters of a shattered chair, like a thick black spiderweb. Two of her front teeth were missing and her neck was broken.

The room was like a cage for animals, but it smelled of people, of human wastes and wasting.

"She's been dead since early this morning," the superintendent said. "As is usual in a neighborhood like this, nobody saw anything, nobody heard anything. She was conducting her ordinary business. Only this one particular client wasn't ordinary. He was—what would you call him in English?"

"Kinky."

"So we have a dead whore, murdered by a kinky client. That certainly seems reasonable, doesn't it?"

170

"I don't know. Whatever you say. I'd like to get out of here."

"Why? You wanted to see her. Well, here she is, take a look ... What's the matter, do you feel squeamish?"

"Yes."

"I knew you were the type. At least be glad you didn't pay for a nice big dinner which you would only upchuck. As it is, you have nothing to upchuck."

Aragon went outside and proved him wrong. The air was fresh, straight from the sea, but all he could smell was the little room and the dead girl and his own vomit.

The superintendent followed him out. "You're becoming a problem, Mr. Aragon. Don't I have enough trouble without a squeamish American on my hands?"

"I think it's a touch of—it must be *turista.*"

"Nonsense. It's murder. You are revolted at the sight of murdered girls. I too am revolted, being a man of sensitivity, but it is my profession to look at them. The eye, the digestive system, the mind, they all make the necessary adjustments. Death is a fact of life."

Aragon leaned against the wall of the building, which was covered with graffiti, mainly in English. The first one he read when his eyes came back into focus was *You were on Canit Camera dummy haha Speedo Martinelli Newark NJ USA*

"Are you feeling better, Mr. Aragon?"

"No."

"You have stopped upchucking."

"I ran out of chuck. I—may I go and sit in the car?"

"Very well. We can talk there."

They returned to the superintendent's Toyota. Even inside the car with the windows rolled up, Aragon could smell the cage that was Tula's room, and with his eyes closed he could see the wall that had served as the community's bulletin board: *This a hell hol ... Chinga tu madre ... Viva Echeveria ... Freddy from Chi ... Hi Freddy ... God Forgive all Sinners ... Constancia 3349 ... Repent ... Lolita está pinchincha!*

"Three deaths," the superintendent said. "And you appear to be the common denominator. You come to Rio Seco to talk to Jenkins and suddenly he is leaping from a bridge. You go away and come back, this time to see Magistrate Hernandez, and lo, he is stabbed by a burglar. You look for Tula Lopez and here she is, beaten and strangled."

"I barely knew Jenkins, I never met Hernandez and I just saw Tula Lopez for the first time."

"But someone knew all those people."

"Yes."

"Someone didn't want any of them discussing him, perhaps telling you where he is. Would you call that a fair assumption?"

"Yes."

"This Lockwood, we must find him."

"Yes."

"Because he is a murderer, a madman."

Aragon stared, heavy-eyed, into the night. The Lockwood Gilly knew no longer existed. He had died somewhere in the years between Dreamboat and the Quarry, and a violent stranger now walked around in his body. "No. No, I can't believe—"

"You must," the superintendent said quietly. "I think it would be wise for you to leave Rio Seco as soon as possible. It is an ugly place to die, especially at this time of year. Spring would be better, when the flowers are in bloom after the winter rains. But one doesn't have a choice of season when one is dealing with a madman. Lockwood doesn't intend to let you find him. That surely is clear to you by now, isn't it?"

"I guess so."

"Naturally, you hate to fail in your mission and thus disappoint your client, but you're young, you have much to live for. Are you married?"

"Yes."

"Your wife is expecting you back?"

"Yes."

"In a box?"

"If you're trying to scare me, don't bother. I'm already scared."

Instinctively, he looked back over his shoulder. The streets were crowded. Rio Seco was opening up for the night.

"No, no," the superintendent said. "Don't look back. He's not there. He hasn't been following you. He's been ahead of you, waiting behind every corner you turn."

"How could he know what I was going to do?"

"I don't mean to be unduly critical, Mr. Aragon, but your actions seem most predictable. That's to say, you're an amateur. Lockwood is a graduate of the Quarry."

Lockwood had learned well—how to con a con man, how to stab as expertly as a surgeon, how to beat up women. Summa cum laude.

"I must return you to your hotel and get to work," the superintendent said. "By the way, have you talked to your rich lady client since our last meeting?"

"Yes."

"You didn't by any chance mention me as a likely prospect for her?"

"No."

"No, of course not. The situation was too delicate. But now you may proceed with a clear conscience, since Lockwood is out of the picture and the situation is no longer delicate. There are a number of facts you might tell her about me which are perhaps not apparent on the surface. For instance, I have never once accepted a *mordida*, or at any rate nothing more than a few cases of liquor. That ought to impress her, yes?"

"Possibly."

"I am a man of honor. I have all my own teeth. Also, I have an independent income, my mother gives me a small allowance. I wouldn't want your client to think I was interested only in her money, when the truth is, I have a very romantic nature. Be sure to mention that."

"I'll mention it," Aragon said. Gilly would need all the laughs she could get after she heard his report: *Your precious B. J. is a nut who kills people, but there's this other guy waiting in the wings with an allowance from his mother and a very romantic nature. How's that for a joke, Gilly?*

"You look peculiar, Mr. Aragon. If you're going to upchuck again, kindly open the window."

He opened the window.

Twenty-two

"Well, this is it," Violet Smith said. "It really is *it,* isn't it?"

Reed yawned, stretched and opened the two top buttons of his uniform. "There's not much point in standing around talking about it. Make yourself useful. Or scarce."

"I'm afraid. I never saw anyone die before."

"So don't look."

"It's different with you, being a nurse. You've probably seen people die all over the place."

"Usually in bed."

"What's it like, watching somebody die?"

"Great fun. Gives me the jollies. Ho ho ho."

"Our minister says there's a moment when the soul leaves the body. When it happens, can you feel it? I mean, is there kind of like a draft as the soul goes up?"

"Who says it goes up? Decker's may be going down."

"Oh no."

"Some go up, some go down, some may even go sideways. Mine is definitely going down."

"You can't be sure."

"Sure I'm sure."

"Why? Are you a terrible sinner?"

"You bet your butt," Reed said, yawning again. "I want to

catch half an hour's sleep out on the patio. Wake me if the old girl starts flinging herself around."

He had been up since four o'clock when Gilly called him and told him her husband was dying. She'd done the same thing a dozen times in the past few months and Reed didn't take it seriously until the doctor came and said it was true. There was talk of moving him into a hospital but Gilly refused. What could they do for him in a hospital—stick tubes up his nose and needles into his veins to prolong his suffering? So he stayed home and she stayed with him.

"He will die in my arms, where he belongs," Gilly told Reed.

"It will be messy."

"Surely you, of all people, should be able to put up with a little mess."

"I'm able. Are you able?"

"Oh God, he's trying to *talk*. I can't stand it. I can't stand his torture."

"See what I mean?" Reed said. "Messy."

Aragon picked up his car at the airport and drove directly to Gilly's house. He wasn't sure how much of the truth he was going to tell her or even how much of the truth he actually knew. With the death of Tula Lopez, B. J.'s last tracks had been obliterated.

He crossed the patio. Reed was lying on a chaise beside the pool, sleeping. In spite of the fatigue circles under his eyes he looked very young and innocent, like a cherub who'd been up all night doing good deeds. Aragon spoke his name and Reed was instantly awake, his voice alert: "What are you doing here?"

"I came to give Mrs. Decker my report."

"Bad timing. The old boy's about to meet his maker. If there's anything she should know, tell me and I'll pass it along to her between fits."

"Tula Lopez is dead."

"Yeah? Too bad."

"She was beaten and strangled."

"That's one of the hazards of her profession."

"I wonder why anyone would bother killing a down-and-out prostitute like Tula."

"For kicks."

"Or money. A nice secure future, let's say."

"You say. I'm going back to sleep." Reed closed his eyes as if he intended to keep his word, but Aragon noticed that the muscles in his forearms were flexed and his jaw was set too tight. "Listen, Aragon, we're all under a strain here right now. Why don't you get lost for a few days?"

"I've been lost. I think I'm on the verge of finding myself."

"Do it some place else."

"No. This is the place I was last seen."

Reed opened his eyes and sat up. "You're talking kind of weird, you know that?"

"I'm feeling kind of weird," Aragon said. "Like a patsy, for instance."

"Yeah? Well, life makes patsies of us all, as my old lady used to say before someone did her a favor and ran over her with a truck. Did I ever tell you about my old lady? She was a fight fan, used to put on the gloves with me when I was six, seven years old."

"You learned early."

"Everybody learns early when they get the hell knocked out of them if they don't."

Aragon watched the plumes of pampas grass bending toward the sun like gilded birds. "It's funny how everyone I was hired to find turned up dead."

"Yeah, that's a real chuckle."

"It would have been simpler and safer if she hadn't hired me in the first place. Why did she?"

"She had to. You speak Spanish, you see, and I don't, except for a couple of words like 'amigo.' Now, I couldn't have gone around looking for Harry Jenkins just saying 'amigo,' could I, amigo?" Reed lay down again, shielding his eyes with his right arm. "Don't worry about anything. I'm not. The Mexican police aren't likely to sweat over the murders of a hustler and a broken-down con man and a crooked judge. They certainly aren't going to bother extraditing anybody. So cheer up. You did a job, earned your money and came out cleaner than Snow White."

"Is that all you have to say?"

"Maybe I'll think of something else later on. Right now I'm

tired and need a little rest. It's a strain waiting for someone to die, even when you don't give a damn about him."

"Do you give a damn about anyone, Reed?"

"Sure I do, amigo. Me."

The drapes were closed, but enough sunlight filtered through so Aragon could see that the oxygen tank beside the bed had been disconnected. Gilly was bending over her husband, her cheek against his. Tears had turned her eyes red and left the lids like transparent blisters.

Violet Smith stood beside the door in her black uniform looking smaller and more subdued than he remembered her. She said, "This is no place for strangers."

"I'll leave if Mrs. Lockwood wants me to."

"This is a sacred moment when the soul—"

"Be quiet," Gilly whispered. "He's trying to talk again. He's saying something . . . What is it, darling? Please, what is it?"

The dying man's mouth was moving and little noises were coming out, wordless croaks and whimpers, and finally, an identifiable sound: "Gee—gee—gee—"

Violet Smith clapped her hands. "Praise the Lord, he's been saved. He's trying to say 'Jesus.' "

"No," Gilly said. "Not Jesus. G. G. He always called me G. G."

"I distinctly heard 'Jesus.' "

"All right."

"I'll go and pray for his soul. O praise the Lord!"

"Yes."

Gilly had not yet given any indication that she was conscious of Aragon's presence.

"Mrs. Lockwood?"

She turned her head slightly in his direction. "They're all dead, aren't they?"

"Yes."

"Do you hear that, B. J.? They're all dead, just like I promised you, like I planned it." There was a long silence, then, "He came back across the border a year ago in a vanload of wetbacks. He was destitute and sick and on drugs. He didn't even have a wallet, but

177

I found an old clipping in his pocket about Jenlock Haciendas, how it was going to be a great step forward for Baja. On the other side of the clipping there was a story about a Marco Decker winning the National Lottery. It seemed a lucky name. He couldn't use his own name, he'd done too many things against the law. So I set up a new identity for him, Marco Decker, and a new marriage for myself, complete with honeymoon in France. I let the word go out, through Smedler and others, that I'd met an eligible man in Europe and intended to marry him. I even arranged for Smedler to send me trousseau money c/o American Express. They sent it back to me in Los Angeles, where I was staying with B. J. in a private hospital. I arranged everything except the stroke. That was real, that was fate."

"Mrs. Lockwood, you don't have to tell me all this."

"You're my lawyer. I'm supposed to be able to tell you everything. Isn't that right?"

"Yes."

"And you're supposed to be able to keep it to yourself. I figured on that from the beginning when I chose you ... One of the nurses in the private hospital was Reed. I hired him to help me bring B. J. home and take care of him. The three of us became not friends exactly, more like allies, allies against fate, against injustice. Reed had had a bum deal too. He fitted in."

She got up and opened one of the drapes slightly. A shaft of sun struck the dying man across his chest.

"There was nothing I could do for B. J. except watch him die, moment by moment, inch by inch. I had such a terrible feeling of helplessness until it occurred to me one day, I don't even remember when, that there was something I could do, after all. I could find the people who corrupted him, who destroyed him, and make sure that they died too. Tula, Jenkins, the judge, they had to die, and they had to die before he did, so I could tell him about it and he would know he was avenged. I told him. He knew."

"Maybe he didn't want to know. Maybe he didn't even like the idea of vengeance. It was your idea, wasn't it?"

"Yes."

"And Reed's work."

"Yes."

"You fed Reed the information I passed on to you. You

178

alibied him by pretending he was here with you when I called from Rio Seco."

There was a sudden movement on the bed, a small final spasm as if the shaft of sun had hit its target.

"He's dead." She sounded a little surprised. "My husband has just died."

He knew she was wrong. B. J. had died a long time ago, in the years between Dreamboat and the Quarry.

THE NEW HARTFORD MEMORIAL LIBRARY
P.O. Box 247
Central Avenue at Town Hill Road
New Hartford, Connecticut 06057
(860) 379-7235

F
MIL

Millar, Margaret.

Ask for me tomorrow.

$8.95   17342

DATE			